Seamus' Girl

Red Eagle Ranch, Book 3

Alyssa Bailey

Love the inside scoop? Sign up for my Newsletter with special offers and bonus content.
https://www.alyssabaileyromance.com

Also by Alyssa Bailey

Red Eagle Ranch
Seamus' Girl

Watch for more at alyssabailey.com.

Seamus' Girl

Protecting her life came at a cost, her heart.

Seamus Red Eagle was a contradiction in terms. If his heritage of Irish and Native American wasn't enough, he was a rancher who flew dangerous missions as a member of the Night Stalkers. When training took him to Hawaii, he met and fell in love with his soulmate, Kailani Aka. When training was over, he left with promises of returning for Kai, but fate had a different path. On the first mission out, he was seriously injured, earning him a medical discharge, a long recovery, and losing Kai to another.

Kai had accepted Seamus didn't love her when he stopped contacting her, but it hadn't lessened her need for him. While piecing her life back together, one family decided they wanted the Aka Ranch. Kai was stalked, harassed, and, nearly kidnapped while fighting to keep her family's land. She went to the only place she knew might help her, Seamus Red Eagle's family.

If ever she needed to hide and seek protection, it was now. But how to enter Seamus' life after his betrayal? She didn't have a choice. When she arrived, he was as bossy and protective as ever. He would take care of her but things were about to get hot... fast.

Series Description

"**Y**ou'll like your brothers again once they each find their true love. Their women will tame them for you."

Young adult, steady job, parents in Ireland for a year, sounds like heaven, right? Not to Saoirse Renee, who is bound by a promise to live at home with her four nosy, intrusive brothers. Their need to run her life with hot Irish tempers and immovable Nakota rules, has gotten completely *out of control.*

Renee, the youngest of five children born to an Irish-emigrant mother and a Nakota Sioux father, often finds reconciling her parents' worlds with her own challenging. The cultural diversity is, at times, explosive. Like this. Richard Red Eagle expected his sons to watch over their little sister, while his wife, Kayleigh, did damage control with their daughter.

With a little help from providence and some strategic orchestrating, Renee intends to help each of her brothers find their true love. She could smell sweet victory and see her freedom just around the corner. Time to get to work.

First victim on the list? The eldest: **Stryker.**

Cover Design by Pro_ebookcovers
Editor: Mary Beth Renn
Manufactured in the United States.

Chapter One

K_ailani_

Kailani Aka looked across the sunlit beach and dreamed of the only man she had ever loved. She should have known that military men didn't stay in Hawaii. Her home state was a place where people vacationed, not stayed. Seamus wouldn't stay.

She remembered the first night she saw him, golden-skinned with his thick, wavy black hair touching his collar and ocean-drenched locks, dripping down his face while carrying his board back to the shoreline. The confidence he exuded was mesmerizing. He was a big man, possibly Hawaiian or Samoan, but there was a distinct quality about him that made him stand out from the others.

He was self-assured and watchful. His eyes met hers when he scanned the beach, and they locked onto Kai. He had a dangerous air about him, and it excited her. Her blood sizzled, and her stomach clenched in carnal desire. Her brain immediately began the mental exercise of getting introduced to, learning, and having fun with him.

This man knew what he wanted and who he was. He appeared naturally comfortable in his skin. Not a military man, then. They often had more bravado and ingrained confidence than ancestral pride. His physical characteristics reminded her of the prevalent Polynesian people of the islands. He drew her attention unconsciously. Her eyes followed him until a half-smile appeared on his face, and he nodded at her in greeting before settling next to people she knew.

Kai fell into her memories.

Wandering over in his direction, a family friend grabbed her arm and introduced them. Kai couldn't believe how much he attracted her. The pull was almost uncontrollable. He drew her to him as though she were the moth and he the fire. His was a strong, fit body, with a distinct pride in himself. That was perfectly understandable, and it was a part of him. Not arrogantly. Assuredly. Boldly.

"Kai, come meet Peter's friend. Kailani Aka, this is Seamus Red Eagle. Shay, this is my friend Kailani."

Looking into his deep blue-green eyes, probably called hazel, they were much more vibrant than any she had seen before. They held a spark and a glow that seemed to mesmerize her. Attracted was a tame word for what she felt when looking at Seamus Red Eagle. Bound. Yes, that was closer.

"Nice to meet you, Seamus."

"Kailani, what a beautiful name. Please call me Shay. Most do."

But he looked like a Seamus, except his coloring fit his last name. His smooth and smoky voice had a depth that danced on her senses, heating her insides, and bringing her spirit alive with expectations of adventure and security. The strength of her reaction to him confused her, yet she knew this man's spirit communed with hers. Indigenous souls that were seeking their kindred life force collided and mingled.

Kailani's grandmother, whom she called Nan, had described the feeling of finding your kindred spirit. This was what it felt like. She could sense the rise of panic. His deep voice swept her off her feet and into his arms. She was his to do as he willed. And by the way, he held her hand for much longer than socially expected, she intrigued him as well. It seemed he could feel the pull. Shay hesitated, but then continued as though they hadn't shared something so intimate that anything else was intrusive.

"Would you like to join me? I haven't eaten in a while, and I'm a big guy. I need fuel."

"Please call me Kai, and I can imagine you'd need lots of it to keep this body going."

He laughed. "Kai, are you saying I'm fat?"

Her face heated. "Big. Sorry, I know it might be rude, but you're impressive." She traced his fit outline with her eyes.

"And now you're checking me out." His voice was full of laughter.

"I am. Do you blame me? No, don't answer that question." She palmed her hot cheeks.

She waited as he made a slow sweep of her assets, meeting his smile when his eyes returned to hers.

"I love that you're checking me out so I could openly check you out. Now, food? Want some?"

"Oh, yes. I'd love some. Red Eagle, is that Native American?"

By the night's end, they had exchanged information, talked for over four hours, and after a bit of begging on Seamus' part, she gave the Irish Sioux a chance. Because of that indigenous connection, he was destined to be significant in her life. Kai believed that now more than ever. And her libido, that had taken a lingering hiatus, had returned like a runaway steam engine going downhill. Unstoppable.

Kai gave herself a pep talk that night as she lay in bed, but no matter how she rephrased her feelings and reactions to the big Irish Sioux, he was hers. He made her think of fierce Sioux warriors and Vikings mixed with persistent Celtic clansmen in tribal splendor. He was a massive bit of delicious contradiction, and she couldn't refuse him easily.

Kailani was never so thankful for her birth control as she was now. She'd rarely needed it as Kai wasn't easily impressed and, therefore, pretty picky about who she took to bed. But she couldn't get the thought of having Shay in her bed out of her thoughts, even though she knew much more about him now.

The next day, when she found out he was indeed a military pilot, she knew he wouldn't stay. She hesitated to ask him why he was in Hawaii, and even if she had asked early in the evening, would it have mattered to her destiny? Probably not.

Kai reminded herself she would never connect with a man who wanted to take her from her island, but now, with Seamus, it didn't seem as important today as yesterday. Her fear said it was heartache brewing. Maybe she had misread things and that perceived connection could be crossed signals, right?

They went to a family party the next afternoon, and Seamus fit right in. It seemed Hawaiian families had a lot in common with Native American families or was it the Irish part? The ethnicity confused her, but the end product was a thoughtful, generous, bossy man. Not her type, she'd thought but entirely her type. Her family noticed and approved. But they didn't know he was in the military. Kailani's Nan smiled at her; happy she had found such a good man. How could she tell her?

"He only watches you, Kai," said her Nan. "No matter where you are, he searches you out. I would keep this one. He even smiled nicely at Seela but then ignored her. If Seela can't lure him away, you have a keeper." Nan had winked at her smiling at the family's inside joke, but she was right. The girl had no shame. Kai's cousin was always trying to get the new guys, even if they were already claimed.

That night, she made her move. If he didn't pass the considerate lover test, she would be done with him, and that would eliminate the dilemma.

"I don't have anything pressing in the morning, Seamus. Would you like to come to my place and hang out for a while?"

Seamus looked at her seriously before nodding his head. "What will your brothers say?"

"I don't know, but it isn't their business, so I'm not worried about what they might say. Are you looking for an excuse to not come over because I'm fine if you don't want to?" She said she would be fine, but she would have been heartbroken if her brothers intimidated him.

"We have tomorrow off, so I can afford to stay up all night."

Kai laughed. "I'm not sure I'm up to that, but I'm open to spending time with you. Lots of time.

Seamus looked around, presumably to locate her blue Subaru WRX. It wasn't fancy, but she loved it. "Did you bring your car?"

"Didn't have to. I live close by. It's better if you take your car though because my place is on Aka property. Here, someone could have it towed or take it home."

"Yeah, it's not worth much, but it is my transportation. I'd like to keep it for the times I need it. Ready to go?"

He placed his broad hand on the small of her back. The finger span covered a considerable space, and she could feel the heat through her shirt. Seamus leaned over as he opened the car door for her. As Kai slipped into the seat, Seamus grinned against her cheek as he leaned over to set her seatbelt.

"Mmm. May I have more?" As he crossed back over, he kissed her hard and fast, then deepened the kiss.

Hot, gently seeking lips caressed hers, gradually increasing the pressure as she tried to reach for more. She unbuckled the restraint to get closer to him. His tongue followed the seam of her lips, and she opened to allow him access. He smelled like a warm musky male, with the clean, crisp scent of a forest and comfort. The dance their tongues engaged in and how he cradled the back of her head was like he enclosed her in a warm, fuzzy blanket of protection.

Then he removed his mouth from hers. She panted hard, dragging in breaths along with him. He pressed his forehead to hers, his breaths back to his typical. Of course, he said he did a lot of training-translated, exercise. Finally, Seamus pulled back just enough to grab the seatbelt again and re-click it into place.

"That was naughty. If daddy puts your seat belt on, you don't take it off."

She grinned at his game. She liked to roleplay. "But daddy was too busy to take it off, and how could I kiss him back if he tethered me to the seat?"

"Brat. I'll address your cute insolence soon."

He dropped another panty-heating kiss and closed her door to walk around and slide into the driver's side of his car.

"What size vehicle do you own... other than this one, I mean."

"Hey, don't insult Betsy here. She takes me wherever I want to go. But when she isn't available," he whispered as though keeping the news from Betsy, "my F250 Pickup works just fine."

Kai laughed. "Backup is always a good idea."

"It is. Now where to, darlin'?"

ONCE INSIDE HER BUNGALOW, Seamus locked the door. "Anything else we need to do? Feed a cat? Walk a dog? Water plants?"

Kai giggled. "No. I live alone. But I'd rather not sleep alone tonight."

"Really? I'd rather you didn't sleep alone tonight, either. But I'm warning you, I like to be the boss. Not every time, but almost. Can you handle that?"

"If you make it worth my while."

"Saucy little thing, aren't you? I might need to show you who's the boss. I brought condoms, but I might not have enough."

"I went to the drugstore, so no worries there." Her smile was feline.

"Did you now? Awfully confident that I would agree, or are you expecting someone who would?"

"Gross. I don't sleep with just anyone. It's been a while since I found some-one to pique my interest."

"I love that I'm the one who gets you excited. It's been about ten months for me. Don't misunderstand me. I gave and received orgasms a few times but not full-on sex. I save that for the ones I really like."

"Glad I'm the one you really like." Her hand slid under his tee shirt and fingers played with his nipples and chest hair. Seamus grinned.

"Oh, sweetheart, you have no idea how much you entice me." Seamus dropped his head and devoured her honey lips.

Walking her backward to the wall, Kai looked up into his eyes, almost black with emotion. Grasping her hands, he raised them above her head, and she immediately squirmed her anticipation. Shay leaned down close, his eyes portraying the passion he held inside. His eyes portrayed raging flames of desire. He possessed her lips, commandeered her mouth, tangoed with her tongue, then kissed every inch of skin on her face and neck.

"Are you getting wet for me, baby girl?"

She squirmed. "Yes, so wet, but maybe you should check."

"I think you're right. We can't be too careful."

He stepped back and smiled when Kailani whimpered and wiggled. She couldn't remember when she had been so turned on. She felt him gently return her arms to her sides, and Seamus rubbed her shoulders. His fingers kneaded the slight ache before dropping a soft kiss in the crook of her neck. Stepping back, keeping his hand on her as she stood taller and stepped away from the wall, he glanced around the room.

Her memories were so vivid that Kai felt the same anticipation she had that night. She wanted him more than she had ever wanted another man.

"Where's your bedroom, baby?"

"Bedroom?" Her processing was slow.

"I'm not taking you over the back of the sofa for our first time, so yeah, where is your bedroom?"

She remembered pointing toward the back of the bungalow and thinking, first time implies the first of many. She could get behind that idea.

Shay took her hand and led the way. He flicked the light and looked in the first room, then continued to the second room, where he added light and entered, confident it was hers. He was right.

"How did you know? They're decorated similarly."

"This room looks homier, lived in. And it smells like you." He led her to the bed and kissed her before he said, "Show me."

"Excuse me? Show you... oh." Her face grew hot. "Um, I like a little foreplay... or a little more of getting in the mood before I take my clothes off. Trust comes into it, too."

"Sweets, this is all about the foreplay. Do you trust me enough to make you feel good, sweetheart?"

He was seriously asking her, and Kailani thought Seamus wouldn't go further if the answer was no or I don't know. She also realized that when it was serious, she thought of him as Seamus, not Shay. Others affectionately called him the warrior Viking, and she could see that side of him now.

Interestingly, they were already creating specific scenarios in which they would do certain things, like calling him by his proper name during significant conversations. The idea of rampant out-of-control, hot sex with the warrior Viking seemed appropriate. All the things couples who have been together for a while would do, seemed natural to them. Another example of how their souls were intertwined on a visceral level.

"I can do that, but then you'll strip because daddy can't get the good stuff started with all these clothes on."

Kai was so aroused she was panting, but she couldn't resist a little tease as it crossed her mind. "I would have thought a man like you could have figured out something." She feigned a dramatic sigh. "Oh, well."

Seamus rolled Kai over and administered three precise but not painful smacks to her ass. She was stunned for a moment, but then the reality that he had spanked her butt slid over her. And a rush of heated excitement followed. He spanked her. She fell further into the role. There was a tinge of embarrassment, but the way her core melted in desire, that emotion barely registered. She gave into the wanton feeling of a protective daddy and the loss of control that realization infused her with.

"Mmm, daddy doesn't like to be teased, does he?"

"No, that was naughty, but what daddy loved was spanking your plump backside. And from the looks of it, you loved it too."

He dispensed with her pants and panties quicker than Kai thought possible. That brought on the intrusive thoughts of jealousy that he may have had way more experience than her, and intimidation joined her thoughts of jealousy.

"What's wrong, baby? You've stiffened. Did I misread the spanking?"

"No. It was nothing. Get back to kissing me. Finish the job, Red Eagle."

"I don't believe you, but I have ways of finding out, little girl."

Kai watched him remove her tee shirt and bra before laying her gently on the bed, completely naked. She knew she had a nice body, but there was still that moment of doubt.

"You are so beautiful. So damn sexy. Perfect."

"I might think daddy was sexy too if I could see him." She gave him a hopeful look, and the man rolled her to her side and swatted her backside again.

"Don't try to take control, little girl. Daddy might take much longer than you ever wanted him to take."

She pouted, but all was forgotten when he reached down to massage her breasts. Kai arched her back, offering herself to him, and watched as his lips slowly descended the long column of Kia's neck, then on to her chest, stopping to pay special homage to her achy breasts, heightening her need. Kissing, nipping, pulling, tweaking one breast while kneading her other breast and then switching his attention again.

Her whimper and little moans of enjoyment slipped from her lips, but she couldn't care because this man played her like the proverbial violin, teasing and finessing her responses. It surprised her, the abandon she felt, but it didn't seem to affect him at all. It was as though he expected it.

His hands were magic, a combination of rough and gentle. The music they made on her body was mind-blowing. His fingers pulled and caressed her nips, then he took them into his mouth... heaven. She tried to influence where he put his tongue, and he would follow her lead sometimes, but other times he would smack her bottom or the side of her exposed thigh, and chastise her for trying to take over. Then he touched her the opposite way on his next contact.

"I'm driving this train, young lady, and you will let me." His voice was playfully firm.

"But I only want to show you where I need you to touch me." Kai had the pleading puppy dog eyes down pat.

"What do you want, baby? Do you want daddy to fuck you or spank you? If you want daddy to fuck you, then you need to stop trying to dictate to me. If you want a spanking, go right ahead, and keep it up."

Seamus had stopped touching. "Don't stop." She sighed dramatically, with a generous portion of desperation. "Okay, fine, do it your way, but you had better not disappoint me." Her words sounded rough with emotion, but her tone was more of a hopeful plea.

"So, fuck you, it is."

Suddenly he made it his mission to get her to climax without touching her clit.

"It won't work." She warned him.

The slap on her thigh was a reminder and an accelerant. She never knew that just that touch of sizzle made her sexy times explode into fireworks. When she simply allowed his hands to touch her, tease her, and explore the depths of her arousal, Kai couldn't control her excitement. Her need brought whimpers. And climaxes. The first one washed over her before she had expected it, and the second came soon after.

"What do you need daddy to do for you, baby?"

She ignored the daddy thing. He was role-playing, but she was too aroused to put any energy in that direction. Daddy in the bedroom was tantalizing, but the new game was too time consuming. She needed more fireworks. Seamus slid one finger inside, and the desperation to come again grew more urgent. She knew men liked that, but she wasn't helpless, just wound tightly in her lust.

"Please?" Begging was no problem if it got her what she wanted.

"Add another finger?" he asked, as he did just that.

She hissed and could feel him touch on just that intense spot inside. Her noises were growing louder as he rubbed all the right spots.

"Could I please come?" Her question was almost a whine of need.

He withdrew his fingers. "Soon, baby. You'll wait for Daddy this time."

He raised Kai's legs to lean against his chest, one on each shoulder, before leaning over to grab a condom from the nightstand. He opened and then rolled the condom on slowly, erotically, while running his thumb through her wet channel.

"Next time, you will do this," indicating the condom. "But for now, I've got one more thing to do before I take you."

He leaned down and ran his tongue through her wet center, and she nearly screamed as her body did mini planks in response to his ministrations Her muscles spasmed hard, her sheath now feeling emptier than when he withdrew his large fingers.

"Seamus, please."

Without a word, he put his cock inside her slippery sheath. He slowly and methodically slid in and out, stopping partway before sliding in fully. He held his position as he breathed and watched her.

"Damn, this is so fucking incredible! Your little pussy muscles are gripping my cock, and the warm, wet welcome... you're paradise, baby, true paradise."

"Less talk, more action. Move, Seamus, move."

He did. Hard, fast, changing his angle to find that spot that would send her to the moon without direct clit action. Kai screamed. Actually screamed, but then she rode the brutal climactic wave that took her out to sea. Seamus groaned and then grunted his release. He kissed her neck behind her ear, and she moaned again, then giggled.

"A sensitive spot. I'll add it to the list. It's becoming quite a long list, my girl."

"Mmm, it tickles. Come lay by me." She smoothed the sheets next to her.

His kiss began hard, then ended softly. "I will as soon as I take care of business."

He handled the condom, washed his hands, and brought out a warm cloth, which he used to clean her up. She'd always had to take care of her hygiene with other guys. No one ever thought to take care of her. She also never let them stay, and Seamus Red Eagle was definitely staying the night.

Kai pulled down the bedding, settled on her side, and said nothing. "If I sleep with you, darlin', you're coming closer. I don't sleep with women, so if I'm breaking my rule, and you are so worth it, then you'd better bring it in."

She whispered sleepily, "Yes, daddy."

She fell asleep with his body wrapped around hers and a kiss on her neck. Nothing could be better than this. If it lasted. But before her thoughts could wander too far astray, Seamus pulled her tighter to him, molding around her so that her head tucked under his chin.

"You are the best thing to have happened to me since I discovered women, Kailani Aka."

Chapter Two

Kailani

K The next morning, it amazed Kailani how rested she felt after several lovemaking sessions throughout the night. And Seamus didn't do one wham-bam-thank you-mam routine. His were full on, two orgasm or a cluster of orgasms before he took his own. She found she liked being on top sometimes, and bottom play was sexy as fuck.

Turning her head she gazed at Seamus' magnificent body, his chest rising and falling minimally. Kai fell in love. He was great in and out of the bed. She admired his muscular frame, seemingly relaxed, yet Kai felt he could and would jump into action at the slightest provocation. Strangely, instead of making her nervous, that comforted her.

Usually, someone built so strong and who was as big a man as Shay, would intimidate her. She wouldn't have been able to relax and certainly not felt comfortable being alone with him for hours, but he didn't do that to her. Seamus surprised her with how perfect of a lover he was. He was in control yet gentle, challenging her hesitations, but not pushing her past them. He led her through them.

Kai remembered that the spanking had been unexpected, and her reaction had floored her. Who would have known that it would be so hot? But it was. She recalled each time he had his release, it always came after she'd had several of her own. Her clit still had the ghost feeling of vibrations, her anus had clenched for moments afterward, and her lips were tender. He had been so attentive and thorough a lover, Kai had been sensitive everywhere the man had touched her.

She often relived the experiences. Her body still throbbed with desire just thinking about that night and all the others that followed. Damn that man.

Seamus turned and ran his hand over her body. "Seamus, I'm attracted, but I'm scared. I'm not sure a military man is someone I can be more than friends with. I'm looking to date with a future." She looked resigned. "I'm not sure that is something I could ever have with you."

"Kailani, expect that I'll do my best to change your mind because I feel a deep connection. I'm sure I won't describe it well, but it's like the stories my Até told us."

"Até?"

"Yes, it's what we call my father. He says there is someone we are destined to meet. They are created for you to be part of your life; I know this is one of those times. It's almost an ancient, inescapable connection. I feel that with you.

"My parents meeting in another country and knowing immediately that they had found their forever. It's like we have known each other for years, just as my father described it. It was almost an ancient connection. I feel that with you."

Kai could only nod in agreement. "I feel it too. So I don't understand why you are in the military."

Seamus laughed and smoothed her lips with his thumb. "If we are supposed to be more than friends, it won't matter where we are or what we're doing now. It will happen."

Kai walked closer and allowed Seamus' body heat to warm her, comfort her, and reassure her. He could do all that and more with his touch. With a look. It was magical. After cuddling for a few moments, she sighed.

"So, how long are you here?"

"Probably for another month for training, then on to Alaska for another level of elite training before I return to active-duty missions."

"So it will be a long time before I'll see you again."

"Not true. I'm a pilot, and I get to plenty of places that aren't me flying a mission on foreign soil. If we continue to feel this way about the other, I'll re-assess my next action plan in a couple of years, earlier if I have a reason to. I don't know what I'll do at that point, but if I have someone that is relying on me, then going home to the ranch may seem like the best alternative."

Kailani was very solemn. "Someone like me? But Seamus, I've never lived anywhere else."

"Exactly someone like you. I hope it is you. But I will eventually go home to South Dakota, back to my family and the ranch. My siblings are all part owners, along with my parents and me. We all have our bits to run, and my parents want to semi-retire in the next ten years. But you have a ranch of sorts here, right?"

"Of sorts?" She blew out an exasperated puff of air. "It is as much a ranch as yours."

"My apologies. I didn't mean to imply that you weren't a full-fledged ranch-er." He chuckled and dropped a kiss on her screwed-up lips.

"With an authentic ranch."

"Yes, I apologize. I know all about pride in place and people."

"Well, you'd better apologize." She said with a sniff. "We have paniolos and cattle as you do."

"Paniolos, those are cowboys. I heard about the history of the vaqueros and paniolos in school many moons ago."

"How do you say cowboy in your native language?"

"My Até has said it before, and believe me, paniolo is much easier to spit out. We have beef cows and buffalo right now, but would like to run a breed of cattle called beefalo. Steer and buffalo breeding is intense enough without adding to the workload so we may not actually go through with it. It's a work in progress and not my job, yet."

Kai chuckled. "We run cattle for the tourists and our dinner table. Buffalo would not work for us."

"Right, but it's indigenous for us, so it makes sense.".

The long history of the Aka family ranch, like the famous Parker Ranch, was a proud endeavor and they spoke of the things they liked about their re-spective ranches.

"The men in my family don't allow me to work the cattle or livestock, and it's annoying. I can ride, but I'm usually relegated to the small resort. It's the old family home repurposed to be a guest house with lots of touristy things outside to occupy them."

"My mother had the same vision, and put Até to work on it. It is now very successful, but it took some years to get it off the ground and to get the word out. Then growing pains, but now, five years out, it's doing great. We actually have what my sister calls 'Duders' for the dude part of the ranch. No resort but a fancy bunkhouse. They don't mind roughing it, but a hot shower and tasty meals are still required after working the ranch."

"Well, we haven't been a resort area as long, but it's easier to advertise things in Hawaii because of this paradise."

"Yes, I can see that would help. Living on the Big Island is honestly unbelievable."

Later that day, after they had spent most of it together, in than out of bed, Seamus returned to his assigned quarters, and she couldn't come back with him. Not that she would have. Shay had responsibilities, but it was hard to see him go. She had a lot of thinking to do before she saw him again. Kailani loved her home, and Seamus loved his. How would they ever find a way?

She thought through some of their similarities. His family and her family had like histories. They clicked. Shay was funny and gentle; strong and sexy. It seemed so right. She knew he would take care of her if called on, so he was probably possessive and protective. After much challenging and begging with herself, she decided she could handle it and sent Seamus a text about where she would be the next night. She couldn't afford to waste any more precious time trying to decide. It would soon be too late to enjoy their time and grow together.

The next day was something she would never forget. It happened after teaching her dance classes to tourists and locals. She grabbed her gear and headed to the meeting spot. It was a nice place called the Soda Shack. It was considerably larger than a shack and served various Hawaiian street foods and beverages. When Kai reached into her handbag to grab her wallet, someone shoved her against the building, and her purse was yanked from her hand.

"Thief!" she yelled, turning to chase him down.

Wearing shoes on the sand dunes made it hard to follow, but a crowd on the beach impeded his progress and allowed Kai to leap onto his back, quickly bringing him down to the sandy earth. The thief would not let the wallet go. She fought harder until he had her on the ground under him.

One slap was enough to still her for a few seconds, long enough for the man to scramble off her, only to be tossed back onto the ground by a tall man. The man's face was obliterated by the angle of the sun. She tried, unsuccessfully, to shield the glare. Strong hands grabbed her and as she got closer, she could see the bulging muscles on arms that pulled her out of the sand to a sitting position. Her rescuer dusted her off while propping one knee, attached to a muscular thigh, on the thief's chest.

"You okay, ma'am—Kailani?"

That voice. "Yes, thank you. Mm, do I know you? This damn sunlight is blinding."

She shielded her eyes again and looked up to view her rescuer, only to stare straight into the solicitous face of Seamus Red Eagle. She stared at the demeanor of a man who had suddenly realized that the woman he had chased behind was his newly acquired lover. Then his face morphed to anger, and she shivered. She cautiously continued to look at him.

He reached a hand down and brought her from sitting to standing in one smooth, firm movement. "What the hell are you doing chasing after this man?"

"Shay, he stole my wallet." Kai leaned down to retrieve it. "And I wasn't going to let some idiot get my stuff. It would take forever to replace all these things."

Seamus pulled zip ties from his pocket and placed them around the man's wrists before fully standing. Kai looked at Shay with amusement, and he shrugged.

"I had a few left in my pocket from training."

Then he turned to look at her full in the face. She cringed under his scrutiny. His lips came down on hers, hard like the waves crashing on the lava rocks. He turned into full-blown chastising mode when he let her up for air.

"Woman, have you no sense? What's your wallet compared to your life? You didn't know had no idea if he was armed or if he didn't mind knocking you out or..."

"Hey man, I don't have a knife or anything," said the thief.

"Shut up." Seamus never took his eyes off Kai's face. He squinted to mitigate the sun's glare instead of pulling out his shades. "Did he hit you? Is that what the red and purple mark is on your face?" Her hand went to the throbbing spot on her cheek.

She shrugged. "Yes? I guess I didn't notice as much because I wanted what was mine." Seamus touched her cheek with tenderness, his eyes sympathetic for a moment before the flames of anger reappeared. To his credit, he did try to keep his tone level.

"Oh, sweetheart, you're going to get a pretty good bruise from this." His protective side went from gentle to censuring again. "We are not done with this conversation, young lady, but I need to kill this guy first for laying a finger on a woman, and touching my woman meant he was contemplating a death wish."

Seamus' breathing was even, but Kailani had difficulty bringing hers down. His woman? She should be screaming, angry with that statement after only a few getting to know you dates and one long sexy evening, but she wanted to be that person to Seamus. She wanted to be connected to him, part of who he was, even for the few weeks he had left. A warm rush of well-being overcame Kai. Shay already felt like ohana to her. He had already ruined her for anyone else.

After they answered questions from the police, they finally got dinner and went to her place. It was almost eight. Seamus had been quieter than the night before. Kai worried he was second-guessing his claim and possibly his attraction to her while she watched him clear their debris and return to the bench table. He grabbed her hand and lifted her chin with his other hand.

Even now, Kai could remember the drop in the pit of her stomach. Could still feel that deep dread when she thought of his seriousness and his words.

"Kai, I meant what I said earlier. I want to consider us together. Is that something you would like?"

"I-I, um... I'd like that, Seamus, but you're leaving soon."

He nodded and took in a deep breath. "I won't be gone forever, Sunshine. That said, I can't have you do what you did today."

"Chase that scum? I had to, or I would have lost my cards, money, information, and phone. It was all in there."

"Kailani, if he had hurt you worse than this bruise, nothing would have stopped me from killing him."

She placed her other hand over his large one. "Seamus. I was okay."

"This time. Promise me you won't do something like that again."

"I can promise to be more self and environmentally aware, but I can't promise I won't try to protect what is mine. I can promise not to put you in a position where you would go to jail for assault."

Seamus grimaced. "Or worse."

Kai nodded. "Or worse."

He fixed her with an intense stare that she felt sure was that possessive, protective side she had imagined. "Because I will paint your ass red with my itchy hand if you do."

"What?"

Seamus watched her eyes grow wide. "You heard me. I'm spanking you the next time you put my girl in danger. You're mine. I know you have doubts, but I don't have any. You're it for me. I have never connected to another like I have connected to you. Don't ask me how I know, but I just know."

And that was when her concept of Seamus came to full knowledge. A hot flush raced up her back and neck into her face. Spanking? How could she be appalled and hum with excitement at the same time? He'd spanked her during sex. Why was this so different? But it was. Seamus kissed her slowly, his tongue sliding between her teeth to duel with hers, raising her need for him while filling another. Seamus was one hell of a kisser, performing the exercise with his whole body focused on the task.

His hands went from tangling in her hair to massaging her tingling scalp. Then they moved on to her neck, her back, where he ran his fingers downward, sending waves of anticipation throughout her body. Seamus grasped her hips as he allowed her air before continuing to anoint her neck and jawline with his magical touch. He then moved his lips back up to hers, and his fingers moved to her ass, kneading the fleshy checks of her backside. His tongue plunged back inside her eager mouth, then lifting her up with his hands on her ass, encouraging her thighs to wrap around his waist.

Whenever their lips touched, the story of an ordinary event became epic. Seamus Red Eagle's lips were always warm like his sun-darkened skin. She imagined that warmth, combined with his mesmerizing blue-green eyes, made for a dramatic response in most women. Kailani was no different from many other women she'd seen behave when Seamus approached. The only thing was, they wanted him. She had him.

If she accepted his proposal of being together. They could melt in his presence, but she had already melded her heart to his. Their spirits had fused. And that was his attraction, his charm, what drew her and others in. It was his watchfulness. People mattered to Seamus Red Eagle.

Sure, it was part of his job, being a member of some elite force, but it was who he was as a person. She'd never had a man give his full attention to her.

Anyone else added her to the priority list, sure, but making her the priority was something she was unfamiliar with. She almost didn't know what to do with all that focus. Almost. But had what changed?

Kailani had to give herself a pep talk about how to conduct herself in his presence. The entire group of elite military men were impressive specimens of humanity. They were civic-minded, as well. That was proven one Saturday, soon after school had started for the children. Local communities put on a neighborhood back-to-school party with school supplies to give away. The guys were great, helping and being good sports about the games.

That night he proved why his friends called him Sharp. He made love to her with laser precision, touching every erotic zone she had ever had. He spent long moments tantalizing her with long, leisurely strokes of his skillful tongue, making sounds of enjoyment that rivaled hers. The memory of how his hands explored every crevice of her body, how he had used his tongue to build her need for him past any she had ever experienced for any man, made her wet. In her experience, which was limited but varied, men didn't enjoy going down on women, at least not like women seemed to enjoy sucking them off.

But Seamus was different. He sucked her clit, and then, instead of bringing her off and ending his obligation to extend his stay between her thighs, he teased, taunted even. Seamus' efforts brought her to completion not once but twice before his head popped up, and he worked his way back up her body, stopping for a noticeable time at each breast. He lavished his attention everywhere he went, and Kai was delirious with the need for him.

"Now, Seamus, I need you inside me before I come again. I have to feel you in me, touching me inside. Please."

"Ah, a sweetheart who begs? What else could I ask for?" He kissed her and shook his head. "I don't want you to ever need to beg for my attention or anything else. I want to know you as well as you know yourself. Help me learn from you, so I never forget while we are away from each other."

Seamus lit up her world then, bringing her to blindingly breathless heights. If a relationship was based on sex alone, they would have been the poster children for success, but it wasn't. There was more to bonding and connection than fireworks of the sensual kind. Many more mundane things like work and responsibilities could and often did bully their way into daily life. But at night, there was little conversation or thoughts of the rest of life's challenges other than how to satisfy the hunger they felt for each other.

She never had another weekend like that again. But she'd relived it a million times. Men were not to be trusted with your heart. She'd learned that lesson.

By the following weekend, Seamus was gone. Since they met, he'd been preparing Kai for him to leave as he wasn't permanently stationed in Hawaii. His team had done training on the big island, her home, and Oahu, along with jaunts to other isles, and all the while, Seamus reminded Kai that he would have to leave, but he'd be back for her. He reminded her how much he wanted her every night with his body and every day with his words. He wanted Kailani in his life because she was his. It would just be harder to prove long distance. His words had begun to fade in her memory, but some she couldn't release. Not yet.

"I can't imagine my life without you, Kailani Aka. I know it won't be easy for you to have a boyfriend who isn't seeing you every day, but I want that. The word boyfriend is too tame for how I feel about you. Once I'm gone, you may have doubts or regrets, so call me. I'll answer if I'm not in training or on a mission. If I don't, it's because I'm out of reach but leave a message, and I'll call as soon as I'm able. If you have any needs, here is my family's phone number at the ranch. Someone always answers. Tell them who you are and what you need. They will make sure it happens."

Before he left that last night, Kailani cut a straight lock of her hair and gave it to him. She produced a locket necklace and a locket keychain.

"Keep this lock of hair to remember me, and I won't cut my hair until we are together again." She placed the bit of hair in the locket and put it on his keyring.

"I can't promise to not cut my hair, but I'm in a job that allows for long hair, so I'll only cut it when I must. I have my mother's curl, so it has to grow a while before it becomes very noticeable."

He handed her a curly lock of his hair and watched as she placed the wavy curl in her locket. The spiral bit of hair lay inside itself as a circle in a circle until a little ring of hair sat neatly in place. Kai had looked at that same lock more times than she could remember, thinking of the man who had given it to her.

Seamus tipped his head to the side.

"What's wrong?" she asked.

"Nothing, sweetheart. I'm trying to envision my Kai with long hair instead of how it is now-short and sassy. It makes me hard just thinking of wrapping my hands in your hair, only longer and thicker, using it to direct you on taking my cock in your mouth. Running my hands through your longer strands of thick, black hair gets me imagining all kinds of things."

Kai lifted a hand to smooth the jaw-length straight black bob she wore now. "Mm, now I'm getting wet. I never spoke dirty until you, Seamus Red Eagle. I'm not sure it's a pleasant side effect of being with you."

"It's a great effect, sunshine. You can visit my home and wait for me any time you want. My family will come to get you or welcome you if you simply show up. I've already told Mam and Até about you. They want to meet you."

"Not now. Maybe someday soon we can go together."

The next day, she went home because seeing him leave the island would have devastated her. It was just aloha, this way.

She prepared to wait for his calls, which came often. At first, she was angry that he had this vital position in the military. Then, when things went radio silent, she didn't worry because he told her he would soon return to his typical job of going on missions. It didn't take long for her to decide to leave her paradise for a lifetime by Seamus' side. She missed him desperately.

Her family had been paniolos, Hawaiian cowboys, for over a hundred years. They had to adjust to the times and make their income by various means on the Hawaiian ranch, so she understood the concept behind Red Eagle Ranch. Seamus' family also owned a huge business that catered to tourists, hunters, and other things like skiing, dude ranching, and cattle. Kai decided she would continue on her family's land until it was time to go with Seamus. Then she would move to the mainland. Until then, work would make time go by fast.

She could wait.

Chapter Three

Five Years Later
   Seamus

Right out of the gate, Seamus Red Eagle was a contradiction in terms. His name brought up visions of good-natured Irish fun, but Red Eagle spoke of ancient knowledge and hard survival in a world he no longer fit. And both would be true and false. A warrior, a Viking god, is what women still called him, even though he rarely entertained anyone of the fairer sex and was even less likely to date anyone.

Seamus appreciated women but wasn't ready to put effort into wooing them since Kailani. His life today was the antithesis of what life had been in the military. That life was full of clandestine meetings and ambushes. He spent years in a rote pattern of brief, go in, do the thing, get out, debrief, take a break, repeat. His last mission closed the career avenue he had lined up, sending him home to a life that was transparent and full of love and family but personally lonely.

Permanency wasn't a possibility until Kailani. He used to love spending time with women of all varieties, never thinking of permanency but having a good time. That was until he met and then lost contact with Kailani. He couldn't get her rich, soulful brown eyes out of his mind, and her smile haunted him. Her body was perfection. Dark, soft, enticing him to give her all she asked for and more.

They had made love to the sound of ocean waves crashing on the rocks or gently caressing the shore. He had mimicked the sea's mood, making rhythmic love bathed in its oceanic symphony. Those days often replayed in his mind's eye.

"Kai, you're not good for me."

"Oh, I'm good for you," she played with the buttons on his shirt. "I'm just not good for your confirmed bachelorhood."

"You're right about that, sweetheart. Do you have designs for ending my single status, then?"

"I have designs on more than your status, ipo."

Her love. He was hers. She'd subtly massaged his bulge while his friends and their dates were busy swimming, and several others were setting up the bonfire. Kailani and Seamus had often found opportunities to sneak off and grab a little loving. Seamus had known he was only temporarily in Hawaii, and falling for Kailani was never what he expected, but she was easy to be with, and love could come so quickly.

When not working, they had spent almost every waking moment and many sleeping ones together for five weeks. When Seamus had to leave, they'd exchanged contact information, promising to connect back up when he was next free. That had been hell. He had wanted to take her with him.

"Kai, let me have my sister fly here and take you home. Or better yet, let me put you on a plane tomorrow. I'll get there as soon as possible, but my Mam and Até will take care of you. My sister Renee and brother Callen will be there too."

"I can't. My grandfather is getting older, and my brothers have families to care for. My father needs my help to care for the ranch."

Seamus made sure she had every family member's number and all the information she would need to contact them for a visit or comfort when a mission took extra-long. Kai had taken every number and programmed them into her phone.

Kailani had left early the next morning to return to the big island and home. She'd said she couldn't see him leave. Seamus had climbed into a C-130 and returned to the mainland, then he and his fellow teammates went to Refuge, Alaska for more training with friends he had met previously. Darrell "Chopper" Frazier, who was now a civilian working some pretty heavy drug and human trafficking rings for the U.S. government, had been waiting for them as they disembarked to the runway sectioned off for that purpose, along with the commander of the training unit, Zayden Wellesley.

Shay enjoyed meeting up with old friends and making a few new ones, and the specialized training was always a challenge, but fulfilling. He had talked about Kailani often in his chats with Chopper, who housed him.

"Man, you have it bad. I know what that feeling is like. It only gets stronger, and you miss her more as time progresses. My recommendation to you," Chopper said as he gazed at his physician wife in the kitchen, "is to figure your shit out and tie her to you as fast as possible. Wait, and it might be too late. The pieces of my life fell into place once I got my head out of my ass and claimed Felicity. Coming to Refuge was the best damn thing I ever did."

For years Seamus went where the Army sent him... this time, it was back to Kentucky, and then off to fly more missions. His TDY to Hawaii was long over by the time his final training had finished, and he was flying missions again.

Shay had intended to step up his commitment after talking to Chopper, who agreed with his Até and his Mam. But when he returned to base, they had less than 48 hours to gear up for the next mission. Free time was officially over. Things had gotten busy fast, and while Seamus loved being active, Kai becoming part of his life changed everything. He wished he was back with her instead. However, Seamus hadn't had much time to dwell on missing her because the mission had been heavy with high stakes and took all his concentration.

That was a long time ago, and he knew it was time to let go because Kailani was likely married now, but for some reason, he couldn't. Shay loved women and enjoyed their company until Kailani, and now that he had lost contact with her, his interest in other women was almost non-existent. He couldn't get over Kai's rich, soulful brown eyes, her passionate responses to him, and how she fit perfectly when she snuggled into him. It was just right.

Seamus still loved the beautiful Kailani. She had seemed to have strong feelings for him, if not love him back, but that was nearly five years ago. They had each other's personal information, but he couldn't contact her because that next mission was the one that got him out of the military within a year. He had been injured - head trauma and broken bones, but he flew his team and the civilians they rescued out of harm's way. Then he'd put down his helicopter on U.S. military soil and passed out. They said he was a hero. He'd just felt broken.

Evidently, it was touch and go for about three days, or so they told him. His parents and Stryker, who had left the military a year earlier, flew to Germany, then followed him to Walter Reed. There was no hiding his injury and recovery from his family. They refused to allow it, and he needed that support.

Finally, his family returned to South Dakota after he promised to go home for rehabilitation after he had healed enough to be released to outpatient therapies. And he did. It did as much for his healing as any formalized physical work did in raising his spirits and bringing him back on track.

Later, when he was healed, and his physical therapy was over, the Army offered Seamus an office job, complete with an ergonomic chair and desk. He considered teaching and overseeing ground school a sweet assignment and strategic operations, which was the second offer.

"It's the best we can offer. You're injuries were too severe to allow you to fly again. I'm sorry."

"Sir, I'm a Red Eagle and flying is what I signed on to do. If I can't do that, it would kill my spirit to sit inside and move around fucking papers. Begging your pardon, Sir. So, I guess I'm going home for good."

His commander reached out his hand and when the men connected, he pulled Seamus in for a manly hug and slap on the back. "Don't ever forget you were the best of the best, Red Eagle. And this man's Army will miss you and your contributions, but never doubt we will always remember your service and sacrifice."

Strategic operations was an excellent job, but not one Seamus wanted. He was a pilot, and because he wanted to fly his missions or nothing, the Army ultimately discharged him with several extra medals for his chest. He never put them on.

Once home, Seamus had been in limbo for a year, and it had been nearly that long since he left the islands and Kailani. Shay hadn't spoken to Kai for close to eleven months, and it hurt his heart. Seamus couldn't forget about Kailani, although he had tried hard to do so for her benefit. When he was well, only left with a slight limp that he was determined to get rid of, he found his thoughts returned to her silky black hair, gentle smile, and dark eyes. His cock's muscle memory of making love to her was so overwhelming, he could bring himself off with just the memory. Soon, thoughts of Kailani occupied nearly every waking moment. The memory of her competed with his nightmares for supremacy. He became obsessed as she occupied every thought.

Later, Shay learned from a service member permanently assigned to a base in the Aloha state that Kai had a boyfriend. No, she was engaged.

"Cassini, are you sure, man?"

"Yeah, I'm sure. Sorry man, I know you and she had a thing, but I figured that was over. I mean because I talked to her fiancé."

"Have you seen her? Is she happy?"

"No, I don't see her around since you left, but she must be happy, right?"

Seamus didn't contact her but kept her info. She said she would wait, but without any word from him for nearly a year, he didn't blame her for looking elsewhere. He had lost his phone in the chaos of moving his things from base to hospital and then to home, so he'd bought a new phone and called it good. He had memorized Kai's number, so finding she had changed her number was like a spear to the heart. He looked up the ranch's number and saved it to his new cell, just to have it near.

She was so beautiful. It was lunacy to think she would hold on until he recovered from his injuries. Injuries she knew nothing about because he didn't tell her. He didn't want her to feel sorry for him. That excuse was becoming old even to his ears.

Seamus hadn't cut his hair because the accident happened on the first mission back. That was nearly four years ago. Seamus didn't know if he would ever get over Kailani and move on. He still dreamed about her at night and longed for her during the day. Até said Seamus might not want to release his memories because she was his destiny. He was rarely wrong, but this had to be one of those times.

Now, he clung to their pact as though it would somehow keep Kailani connected to him. Possibly even lead her back to him. His grandmother always said love was powerful medicine. He'd hoped she was right, but the way his life was playing out, it wasn't strong enough.

After a few years, he'd dated unsuccessfully because, honestly, when you've had perfection, the rest would always lack in noticeable ways, sometimes in many ways. He was screwed unless he could let go of his obsession. He'd called Kailani's parent's home annually since he learned she was engaged. He had never spoken to anyone but a random employee who answered the phone. It was time he gave up.

One last call. One last attempt at connecting with Kai before he deleted the number and filed the memory with other unfulfilled desires. His depression was falling like a heavy brocade curtain, obliterating, and muffling the pain. His scream of injustice was building.

Maybe he'd try those damn antidepressants that Jocelyn O'Connor, a friend of his father's childhood who now lived with her husband and his large family in Elk Ridge Montana and Sheridan, Wyoming, had suggested. The VA harped about them every month when he went to the counselor. If he got bad news, and if the person on the other side of the line left him with no hope, he wouldn't call again. He'd start looking for someone somewhere else. Possibly Rapid City, where there was a little more population.

Seamus called his cattle dog, Maverick, to heel. That dog was the most loyal and protective animal he'd ever known. Renee had said Maverick was like his owner, gentle to a fault but possessive and protective of what was his. Maverick rarely showed his teeth, but when he did, there was a good reason for it. Just like his owner used to be. Seamus doubted he was even close to the man he was when he left college.

Stryker slapped Seamus on the back as he walked into the family room. "Hey, Bro, we're going to Cattleman's. Go with us."

Seamus shrugged. Might as well start living. "Yeah, I think I will. Let me clean up and make a quick phone call. I'll meet you out front in twenty."

"You got it."

Chapter Four

Seamus

S In his room, Seamus pulled out the phone number he had kept in his wallet since leaving Hawaii. Punching in the 808-area code, he hesitated before putting the next seven numbers in. It took a couple of seconds to connect.

"Aloha. Aka Ranch and Resort."

"Yes, may I speak with Kailani Aka?"

"I'm her Nan. Who are you?" demanded the elder. "If you're with that worthless Paolo family, you can stop calling. We aren't selling, and you won't find her."

Seamus chuckled a little. Kai had said her grandmother was plain speaking which was fine with him. He'd had more than his fair share of liars working on missions. He could respect that.

"No, ma'am, that isn't who I am. This is Seamus Red Eagle. I'm a friend of Kai's." The word friend almost stuck in his throat. He'd thought they were so much more than friends, but it'd been a long time, and he could only hope she'd still see him as a friend.

"You're the pilot?"

"Yes, ma'am, that's me."

"I don't like you. My granddaughter suffered when you didn't come for her. I don't like that."

The thoughts that ran through his mind were crippling for a second before he put his head back in the game. Don't mess this up. "That's fair. I understand, ma'am, but I was injured. Then when I got home again, I learned she had a fiancé. I don't mean to cause her trouble. I just want to speak to her."

"Who told you... Oh, that boy? He isn't a child, but he acted like one when he didn't get what he wanted. Our ranch. My Kailani was never interested in a boy, and she would never marry no one but you. Why didn't you come back? She wouldn't be having this trouble if you had come back."

The accusation was more than clear. She didn't blame Kailani's Nan for her thoughts. He'd screwed things up, and it was up to him to fix it. Hearing Kai wasn't engaged or married and had never been made him lightheaded.

Seamus smiled at the way of speech some older Native Hawaiians had. "As I said, I thought she was engaged, and I didn't want to complicate her life."

"If you wanted her, you'd be here now. You would have been here four years ago trying to win her back, not being Mr. Considerate. Now you get my granddaughter and fix this. You have to glue her broken heart back together. Don't call me back until you do."

She sounded as though she was going to hang up. "Wait, Mrs. Aka. Where is Kailani?"

"She went to fix her heart. Don't you have her?"

"Have her? No, ma'am, or I wouldn't have called looking for her."

Old Mrs. Aka laughed. "Yes, I guess that's true." Then she was more somber. "She left to escape that idiot who thinks he can have my family's ranch by having my granddaughter. He has no smarts, that one, and he's pushy. So when you find my granddaughter, tell her don't come back until I tell her it's safe. And you take care of her."

"What's his name?" Seamus' tone dropped even lower. "I'll be on the next flight out."

"Mmm. Yes, you'll do for my Kailani. Don't worry about Rufus Paolo. His people don't have the close ohana like we do. We can handle things if we know Kailani is safe. Besides, if you come here, who will take care of her?"

"I promise you I'll find her and keep her safe."

"And make her happy."

"Yes, ma'am. I'll make her happy if she will let me." Kai's Nan rushed off to see to a guest.

He hoped he could make good on that promise. Kailani was coming here? Damn. He forgot to ask when she'd left Hawaii. He called the elder back to see if he could get Kai's phone number and when she left, but the employee that answered said she would pass on the message. Since Mrs. Aka wasn't worried she hadn't arrived yet, maybe Kai had just left home. He'd have to wait her out.

"Seamus, you coming? We're starving," Carter called up the stairs.

"Yep, I'm almost ready."

Shay headed into a three-minute shower and used up another three minutes redressing. He grabbed his hat, slipped on his boots, and checked for his wallet and phone before walking out the front door. All the while, he thought about his Kailani being in danger. Yes, she was his, and yes, he planned on claiming her and marrying her as soon as she let him. But where the hell was she?

As he climbed in his truck, he took good-natured ribbing from Carter and Callen about taking longer than a woman. Renee hit Carter in the back of the head.

"I'll have you know that I don't take long to change or get ready."

"If you say so, sugar." Carter ducked to avoid the next swipe at him.

"Don't call me that." Renee had a mutinous expression on her pretty face.

Carter laughed. "Okay, Miss Prickly Pear."

She smacked him again, causing Carter to laugh harder as he palmed his head. Unable to come up with a suitable comeback, Renee sat grumpily in the seat.

Once they arrived at the community's version of a gathering place, the women grabbed two tables and pushed them together. Forrest, the majority owner of Cattleman's, gave the women a raised eyebrow. Renee shrugged and set up enough chairs for all eight of them.

Renee said, "I'd hoped Tansy would show up, but it doesn't seem they're going to make it."

Avery patted Renee's hand. "There's still time. Even if she doesn't make dinner, the music, and dancing last into the night."

"I guess, but I said to come for dinner."

"I get it because. I called Janna too. I think she's still irritated that I got one of the Red Eagle men without planning to do it. She's set her hat for Seamus, but he doesn't even look her way."

"Are you going to try a little Avery magic?" Teagan asked.

"What, to get Janna and Seamus together?" Avery shook her head. "Oh, no. I got my Red Eagle the hard way. If she wants one, she has to make it happen. Besides, I don't think that Seamus is looking. And even if he was, Janna tends to step over the line too often to ever sit comfortably again if she had a Red Eagle man."

"Yes, that would get old fast for both of them." Renee flattened the napkins as she pulled them from the dispenser.

The waitress spilled a little water on the table. "Oh, I'm so sorry."

Renee shook her head. "Don't worry. It's only water."

Teagan smiled. "No worries at all. We're having ribs, and the tablecloth will come off anyway."

The gorgeous, willowy woman cocked her head to the side. She was of average height but gave the impression of being much taller with those long legs and torso.

"But if you leave it on, there isn't as much work cleaning the table later."

"But it will stain the tablecloth, right?" asked Avery.

"Pfft. These are restaurant-grade tablecloths, so they're made for heavy washing."

"Okay then, we'll leave it on." Teagan smiled at their waitress. "Are you new to town?" Cattleman's didn't have nametags on their employees. "What's your name, if you don't mind me asking?"

"Kai. Thanks for leaving the tablecloth. Now, can I take your drinks order?"

The beautiful woman had such an exotic look that Renee expected she was aboriginal or something like that. Not an Australian accent or European. No, she looked different, but she couldn't place her nationality. It would be rude to ask right after meeting her. She'd ask her the next time they came to Cattleman's.

"My brothers are supposed to be getting things set up, but if you could stop back by in a bit, I'm sure we'll need refills. Thanks, Kai."

As their waitress moved off, Teagan nodded toward the door.

"Or maybe they have new friends."

"What? Who?" Renee jerked her head around and saw Janna and Tansy with two strapping young men. Avery cocked her head to the side.

"Aren't they the Thompkins twins?" Avery hummed. "They're hot in stereo."

"Yep, but they're double trouble," said Renee. "Brian and Brady."

Teagan got up to grab two more chairs and did a quick head count before grabbing table number three. She didn't dare look over to where she last saw Forrest. He was likely standing with his hands on his hips. He could totally rock the "that's a terrible choice" look, and it sometimes rivaled Declan. Teagan occasionally wondered how many of the guys that went to high school with the Red Eagles have that demeanor. The woman Forrest ever settled on would have a lot to contend with. Teagan hoped the future McGregor woman could weather the rough storm that was Forrest McGregor.

Seamus sent Teagan to sit while he finished setting out chairs.

"I'm almost done, Shay. Let me finish."

"I can see that, and no. Go sit down and don't sass. I'm in the mood to swat a few asses tonight."

"Hooking up tonight, Seamus?" asked a too obviously hopeful Janna. "You know, to relax you," she tried to explain ineffectually.

"No. And with the men you two walked in with," he looked over at the bar where the men were placing their orders, "I'd be surprised if either of you will, either. Those guys are already trolling just standing at the bar. They're going to either get in a fight for trying to claim someone else's date or claim another woman and take her home." The women looked over; sure enough, those yahoos were bumping hips with several servers.

"Mind your own business, Seamus Red Eagle. They're just being friendly," said Tansy. But the look on her face said something else.

"Yeah, that's a little too friendly for men who brought dates, in my book. If you need me to kick them to the curb, just let me know. I'll enjoy it. And don't let me see you defending men who don't respect women. Especially those associated with this family. And before you say it, young lady, I mean both of you. Best friends count."

Seamus lifted his eyebrow at Janna and Tansy, then turned away, winking at Avery when he caught her eye. She pretended to fix the napkins on the table, likely to hold back a grin. But Shay meant every word. If these women were good friends to his sister and almost sisters, they were part of his protective circle. He'd at least keep an eye on them and if they wanted to dump the twins, that would work, too. He was spoiling for a fight.

Just as he sat down, he saw a woman weave between the tables and could have sworn it was Kailani. Hell, now he was seeing things. His groin tightened in remembrance of her sassy sweetness. He might have introduced himself if it weren't for his conversation tonight and the new information he had just received. All this thinking about Kai and her own asshole was making him hypercautious.

"What's gotten into you, bro?" asked Callen. "You're normally more easy-going."

Seamus shrugged. He wasn't going to give away information about his phone call. He'd cross that bridge with the family when and if he found Kailani. He had to admit that she might not be coming in his direction, so all his newly acquired information was unconfirmed until he saw her. His heart didn't hesitate to leap a little in anticipatory desire. Maybe he could fix it with her after all.

"Nothing. Tired of assholes, I guess, and tired of not getting any satisfaction when I deal with them."

Carter nodded. "Sometimes it seems like assholes rule the world."

"Not on my watch, they don't," said Stryker.

Callen smiled as he looked over at Brian and Brady before returning to the group. "These days, they at least provide entertainment."

The occupants of the table laughed, but Stryker didn't crack a smile because he didn't see the humor. Seamus could see both sides. The assholes made obviously stupid moves that lightened the mood, but he got where Stryker was coming from. It had been a difficult time when Avery's brother had gambled not only money he didn't have but his sister's life.

He'd done whatever he could to meet his debt obligations, using his sister, their family farm, and the Red Eagle Ranch as payback options. Avery had been hurt in the process. Putting his girl in danger was something Stryker would never let happen again if it was in his power to stop. Still, they all acknowledged that the situation could have gone south quickly if her brother hadn't been dealing with family.

Then there was Teagan and the difficulty with her stalker. It was terrifying for the girls and drove the brothers to take drastic measures to ensure Avery, Renee, and Teagan's safety. Then, there had been his accident. The one that got him medically discharged.

He still hadn't told anyone the details concerning that final assignment. Those events leading up to and surrounding his last mission, the injuries, and his subsequent depression, compounded by his refusal to have his people around him until he was fully recovered. That entire event had haunted him often until he'd learned to put a lid on the devastation and the horrors that clusterfuck had been.

"I think keeping the crazies and the idiots out of our domain is the soundest decision for us. We've dealt with enough lately," said Seamus, fearing another round was just around the bend..

"Guess we have to keep a tight rein on our corner of the world then," said Callen.

His youngest brother didn't know how right he was. Seamus knew he was different when he'd returned home, bringing with him his emotional ball and chain from the things he had seen and done over those years. The whole family noticed, and each of them had their past to make peace with, but it was something he might've let go of more completely if he hadn't thought he'd lost Kailani to another man.

After the accident, Seamus resisted calling Kai from the hospital because he didn't want to bring her a broken man. He had waited until he was strong again; had proven he could work the ranch, pull his load, and be the man she needed, that she deserved. A man that was capable of giving her a night of loving like he used to after managing a day's work. That had taken at least a year, and he regretted that decision every day because he'd lost her.

But if what her grandmother said was true, that might not be the case. Although Kai could have hidden the truth from her Nan, Seamus doubted it. Kai was honest to a fault. No, he was sure she was coming here if that's what she'd said. But when?

Seamus heard laughter and tuned back into the conversation that had continued around him.

Avery grinned at her broody, too-serious man. "Should I put that in a memo, honey? No assholes allowed on the ranch?"

Were they still on that subject? It seemed like hours since they started it. Stay in the moment, man.

"Hell yeah, if that works." Stryker wrapped his hand around the back of her neck possessively and kissed her breathless. "This makes me feel better." He kissed Avery again.

Seamus' gut clenched whenever he saw Stryker and Avery radiate their love for each other or when Declan and Teagan made a demonstrative declaration of love and possession. He'd had that with Kai, and dammit, if she came here for a safe haven, he would give it to her, but at a price. She'd have to accept his need for her, that he still loved her. Seamus had never told her he loved her, but it was understood. Wasn't it?

Declan grinned. "Hell, yeah. Kissing always makes things better." He leaned into Teagan to make his point.

Renee laughed. "Problem solved."

Seamus grunted and mumbled something about kissing her butt with the palm of his hand.

"Rude," was his sister's response.

That made him smile as he bit into a tender beef rib. Good food. Just what he needed. Seamus couldn't get the phone call with Kailani's grandmother out of his mind. The older woman was feisty, that was for sure, but even she sounded like Kailani needed help. Just who was this fucker anyway? Messing with his woman was the wrong thing to do if he wanted a long life. If that Rufus Paolo guy came close to Kai, that is what Shay would happily teach the loser.

And why had he been told she was engaged when she wasn't? He'd be having a serious discussion with Kailani about things but not until he found her and made sure she was safe. Once that happened, he'd get the whole story, whatever that story was.

Maybe he would call her Nan back tomorrow to find out when she left Hawaii. The thought flitted across his consciousness that Paolo could have followed her. He might, even now, be holding her against her will. Seamus shut that shit down because it did no good to borrow trouble.

But one thing was for sure, she had come here for protection, and even if she wasn't looking for him, she was looking for his family to help her. Whether or not she wanted to admit it, she'd come to the right place. He hoped her Nan was right because now that the possibility of Kai needing Seamus' help had surfaced, he could think of little else but claiming her. He was ready to wrap his arms around her, protect her, sink into her heat, and take possession. This time, for good.

He got more ribs and maybe see if he could find that waitress because he was sure he hadn't seen her before. Not that people didn't come for the summer and holidays, but if she was a server, then he wanted to know who she was for his own peace of mind. Was that her? He stood and headed in that direction.

"Seamus, why are you so distracted?" asked Renee. The concern in her voice was obvious.

"I'm fine. Just hungry and maybe wondering what my next life move is. Don't ask, that is the most I'm sharing, but I love you for asking." He hugged Renee, who hugged him back. "I wonder if we could get a pitcher of beer. Do you know where our server is?"

Renee looked around and pointed out the long-legged beauty he had spied earlier. The woman who reminded him of Kai. Kailani? Of course it wasn't. She wouldn't be serving in Cattleman's, but she intrigued him and if Kai didn't show up, he might want to explore this luscious woman.

"I'll grab her."

Chapter Five

Kailani

Kai finally returned to the engaging women's table after they had all been eating for a bit. She wished she had a group of friends like these women. She did once, but after spending most of her last year hiding from the Paolo family, that closeness had waned. Kai was exhausted and she had several more hours to work. She'd been pampered, working for the family business and she readily resolved, she'd never work for anyone outside her family again.

She'd been so run off her feet tonight, so she didn't have a chance to see the men at the ladies' table, but something told her they would be impressive. They must be with powerhouse women like these. She remembered this was a family in the making. The brothers of one were the other two's boyfriends.

A few extra couples had shown up in the meantime, but they didn't have the same presence as the original three.. Kai could tell that even from the way across a crowded warehouse-sized room. She had hoped to meet the men in the family but was disappointed when she arrived at a nearly deserted table. Maybe they had gone home already.

At Cattleman's, she drew lots of male attention, including from several who now sat at the end of this table. They seemed uncomfortable and obviously related to each other. Not the men to the women she'd just met, then. Kai was sure that the men in Renee's family would have more presence, more put together than these two appeared to be. Kai watched a well-built cowboy lean down and talk to the men who argued, then got up from the table with their beers.

Kai mentally shook her head. Why she'd chosen to work first instead of just show up at the Red Eagle's ranch was something she asked herself every night when she went home with tired feet, bruised butt cheeks, and immensely weary of dodging handsy, inebriated men.

If Seamus knew she was putting herself at risk this way on purpose... her body shuddered at what he would do. No, she reminded herself. That was the old Seamus. The one who put himself at risk to keep her safe. That was the gruff man with the tone to match if she did anything that drew unwanted attention to her or placed her in uncertain situations.

He had changed. He must have changed to have stayed absent from her life. What if he was home now? Would he send her away? She'd never even considered that, and her belly seized. She couldn't afford to entertain those thoughts now. It was too late to change her course. Seamus may not love her, but he was a man of honor and integrity. He would turn her away for doing as he had said.

She knew why she had gotten a job first. She wasn't ready to see Seamus face to face after no contact. Plus, she needed money and some place to stay instead of the sleazy motel she was at. If she just put up with crap a little longer, she'd have enough money to rent a tiny place and then go to the ranch. She had money but getting a job was an excellent strategic move. She wouldn't look needy when she called on the Red Eagle Ranch, which was important.

When Kai first arrived, she'd worried about the possibility of Shay still being in the military. The owner, Forrest McGregor, was a nice guy, and he was generous to hire her when she didn't have experience in this specific job. He told her Seamus had been home "for a while." That settled it. Seamus didn't want her, but his integrity might still allow him to help her. She had no other safe options.

"Hey, ladies, just a couple of you left?" Kai asked, nodding at the mostly empty chairs.

Avery smiled. "Nope. We're all here, well, except for the jerks sitting with our friends at the end of the table. Callen invited them to leave with all their arms and legs intact. They decided it was time to go... home, I hope. Twins." Avery shook her head. "The rest are dancing. I'm here waiting for my guy to come back from the gents. One is picking up our next order. These men can eat. I'm Avery, by the way."

"Nice to meet you, Avery. I'll just ask the women at the end of your very long table if they need anything."

"Yeah, that's Janna and Tansy. They aren't too happy with how tonight has turned out. They may go home soon, too. And don't worry, we'll return the tables to their original spots when we leave. Forrest doesn't like us to do this, but how else can we enjoy each other's company? Anyway, here comes Renee and Carter. They're arguing again." Avery grinned. "Lovers' spat, but don't tell them that. They haven't figured it out yet."

Kai smiled and nodded as she sidestepped someone obviously intent on connecting with a person at a table on the other side of Kai. Renee stepped around Carter when she spied Kai.

"Hey, you made it back."

"Yeah, sorry it was so long. Some guys get too much to drink and get familiar... too familiar, if you get my meaning."

Carter looked concerned. "If you need me to set anyone straight, you let me know. I'm Carter, by the way." He reached out his hand.

"Nice to meet you. I'm fine. Everyone seems to know there's a line, but some like to walk it. Maybe I should have gone and tried The Watering Hole."

The group murmured their disagreement. "Not there. Our guys would have dragged you out of there."

"But they don't know me."

"They would have found out a lady was over there serving and would have taken you out. There is a reason there are mostly men working there. It's worse than here with handsy guys. Actually, this is usually a nice place. If you tell Forrest, he'll send the ones who have had too much to drink home. But at The Watering Hole, the seedier clientele shows up, and no one cares how drunk they are as long as they keep paying. This is much better," said Renee.

"Besides, most men here wouldn't allow you to deal with crap like that. They'd either get Forrest or encourage everyone to play nice. I mean, if you were manhandled, not just flirted with," added Teagan as she and Declan returned from the dance floor and settled back into their seats. "And this is my fiancé, Declan. Dec, this is Kai. She's just moved to town and is a server here."

Declan shared a devastatingly beautiful smile. That smile looked familiar. "Kai, nice to meet you. Watch hanging out with this rowdy brood of women. They will lead you astray." He dropped a sexy kiss on Teagan's lips. He placed an order for another pitcher of beer and one pitcher of margaritas. "That is all you get, ladies, so go easy."

Teagan pouted. "But we aren't driving."

Declan leaned into his girlfriend and said something in her ear.

"Oh, right. No more for me," said Teagan.

She grinned broadly and turned a little pink, leaving little to interpret as to what he said. Sexy times were ahead. Kai sighed in memory of her and Seamus. He had been demanding, and he had always satisfied her.

Avery smiled at the drop-dead gorgeous man that stopped behind her and slipped his hands on her shoulders to massage her muscles. Avery moaned her appreciation.

"That feels so good. It rivals sex."

The man leaned down and said something low in Avery's ear. She blushed hard. Kai's belly clinched in remembrance of another sexy man with magic hands and whispered admonitions and promises in her ear. How could her attraction and yearning for a man last so long and stay this intense? Because you wanted him that badly. You fell for him. Too bad he didn't feel the same as you, no matter what he said.

"Kai, this is my man, Stryker."

"Stryker? That's an unusual name. I've only ever heard it once."

Didn't Seamus say his brother's name was Stryker or something? Maybe she remembered it wrong, or perhaps it was more of a regional name here.

"It is uncommon. I only know one person with it, me. Where did you hear it from?"

"Someone I knew a while ago mentioned a relative with that name."

"Who? I might know them."

Kai tried to laugh it off. "I'm not from South Dakota, so I doubt it."

She felt her heart flutter when Stryker grinned at her. Her Seamus had a smile like that. Seamus' smile was devastatingly handsome, too, taking his face from attractively fierce to gorgeous. A definite pattern emerged. Pull it together, Kai.

"Fair enough. But I was in the military, so I've been around the world a few times."

"Ever been to Hawaii?"

"No. But my brother has. Is that where you're from?"

"Yes." This was becoming uncomfortable.

"Well, you're here now, darlin'. So if you need anything, just call one of the girls, and we will take care of you." He looked sheepish. "Sorry, not exactly what I mean. The girls will care for you, but they have us for the muscle." He got more serious. "Don't forget to give them your number before we leave tonight."

"Thank you, but I'm sure I won't need it."

"You never know." Stryker looked at Renee and then Avery, who smiled at Kai. She was pretty sure that she'd be giving them her phone number before the group went home.

One twin passed behind Kai and pinched her butt. "Ow!" her hand went back, and her thundercloud face turned to the jerk who'd done it and met a twin grinning. Were these men only children? And wasn't that the girl he came in with? She almost clapped when she heard the woman in question address the jerk.

Tansy elbowed him hard in the side. "Our date is over, asshole. I thought you'd have gone home by now. I'll be sure to tell my friends about your dating ethics."

"What do you expect when you bring me to a table full of Red Eagles? A man's pride can only take so much."

Brady Tompkins stormed off, snagging the first girl he passed, and headed to the dance floor. His date had already dismissed Brian, but all that caught Kailani's attention was the name Red Eagle.

"Red Eagle?" asked Kai.

At just that moment, she tried to sidestep a man stumbling past and lost her balance, landing against a hard chest. Her tray clattered against the chair next to her, hitting the floor unnoticed by most in the bar. She mentally sighed, then focused on where her mind had first gone, Seamus.

"Oh, I'm so sorry. I guess I zigged when I should have zagged," she said, flustered.

This man smelled like soap, with a sharp tang of evergreen and male musk that she knew intimately. Damn, this was his family. This was him. Brawny arms came around her, holding tight when she teetered. Kai nearly let herself relax into his familiar protective hold. She'd missed this.

Renee attempted to pull her away from Seamus, the one she once called her man. The one who held her steady, once upon a time.

"Leave her to get her bearings, Saoirse Renee."

Oh, God. That was his irritated voice. Kai shivered. This intense growl had to be his. She inhaled his scent deeply and then released her breath. She was in the arms of the man she had dreamed about and pined over for so long. The same soldier whose kisses had taken her very soul and who made her believe he could love her. But he didn't.

"Don't be such a brute, Shay. This is Kai, and she isn't used to men like you."

Yep, no doubt now. Kai stepped back slightly. It was the only amount of space Shay would give her.

Renee continued to speak. "And this is my brother, Seamus. I'm sorry he's acting like his ancestors. He really does know the modern expectations of social niceties. Shay, let her go."

At first, Kai dreaded stepping back against his hold, forcing his arms apart to release her, but then anger took over. He was home and never tried to contact her. She had felt the same outrage when Forrest said all the Red Eagle boys were home. They'd returned in "full force." The asshat. She leaned back far enough to throw him a sizzling glare.

Her tummy danced and carried the party further south. Damn her body. Shay pulled her close again, dropped a kiss on the top of her head, and gave her arms a little squeeze.

"God, I've missed you."

Kai stepped back when Seamus lessened his grip. The corner of his mouth ghosted an upward tilt before vanishing as though he'd never reacted. She surveyed the man she couldn't get out of her mind. She remembered his kisses, gentle lovemaking, and passionate fucking in an avalanche of memories. But he'd changed, or maybe that wasn't ever him.

He was leaner, stronger if that were possible, and something else. Sadder. Life had pounded on him since she'd last seen him. Something had happened to give him that darkness that crossed his eyes for a brief second before it was gone. She'd barely registered it, but the feeling was still there. Take the shadows that seemed to lurk so close to the surface. She wanted to ease his pain. And she wanted to scream at him. She was a basket case.

"Seamus, please." She pleaded with her whole body. They locked eyes as she watched him.

He was edgier, more intense, and more determined than the man she had grown to love all those years ago. To those who didn't know Shay, he could often appear dangerous, but now he gave off a lethal aura, a kind of subliminal warning that messing with him was not a good idea. She shivered involuntarily.

Seamus' granite voice broke through his sister's chattering. "Saoirse, back off. Kai and I know each other already."

A frisson of caution ran through her at his coldness. Seamus' tone was ominous, but his touch was gentle. His hand caressed Kai's upper arm possessively. Renee must have noticed because when Carter, the man she had been dancing with, pulled on her arm, she allowed him to lead her away.

The need to justify her presence, her reasoning for not telling him she was here, hit her hard. "Seamus, I can explain."

His finger went over Kai's lips. "Hush, sweetheart. I'm processing this mess and need time to work through everything. God, I've fucking missed you."

"Missed me or fucking me?"

He relaxed and grinned. "Both, naughty girl, but daddy doesn't allow that kind of talk. You have already earned a spanking."

"What about you?"

"What about me, sunshine?"

His voice was too low for anyone to hear, but Kai glanced around anyway. She caught Forrest's frown in her direction.

"Look, I have to move to another table, or I'll get fired. I'll see you later."

Chapter Six

Seamus

Seamus stood in disbelief that Kai had thought working tables manned by hungry cowboys, some hungry for more than food and drink, was a better alternative than coming to him straight away. He knew she wouldn't lose her job, but he didn't want her to have it His mind was already processing that he could publicly stake his claim for her protection if she didn't quit. The thought of another touching his Kai was more than he could handle.

It was true that he didn't know her like he used to, but she couldn't have changed that much. Seeing Kailani earlier and thinking he saw things, wondering if it was her, was nothing compared to the shock of realizing he held her in his arms. It brought longings slamming back, taking his breath away, driving a deep pain in his gut. Thoughts and feelings he'd tried to bury because he thought he'd lost Kailani came back in full force.

Working at Cattleman's was not okay. She'd need to quit. Seamus had sunk a portion of his savings into this establishment and kept an eye on how it was run. It was a respectable place by other cowboy club standards, but not for his girl. Except his Kai was a stubborn woman. It was one of the things that attracted him to her in the beginning, her sense of self. And the area they most battled over.

He didn't understand why Kailani was here. It seemed irrational when she could have just come to the ranch, but it was a question among many others. Questions like: was she married to that Paolo guy? He went back over the conversation with Kai's Nan earlier this evening and found he wasn't sure. Had she ever been married? No, if not this Paolo guy, she hadn't married anyone.

And if she was looking for Seamus, then why did she get a job here instead of coming straight to him? She wouldn't. Things weren't adding up. He'd let her work while he processed the information and plotted his next move. He sat back and watched her.

Seamus gave into his family and answered a couple of probing questions posed by the girls and then said, "Enough."

His brothers must have reinforced that one word because the girls didn't argue... much. Avery leaned into Stryker, who kissed her hand and listened to whatever she had to say. After a couple rounds of responses, he frowned and kissed the top of her head before rising and sitting on the far side of his brother. Seamus frowned.

"Whatever you want to say or that your Avery wants you to say, don't."

"Well, see, that poses a problem."

"Not for me," answered Seamus.

Stryker grinned. "Possibly, but Shay, listen man. You would rather hear me jawing at you like a brother than Avery talking to you like your sister. Trust me, she has a way of discussing things that make a man give up and give in as the lesser evil."

Seamus gave his brother the side-eye, keeping his primary focus on Kailani. "Sounds like Avery has you wrapped around her little finger."

"Yep, she does indeed. I think that sweet girl you are staring at so intently has you likewise tethered to you."

Shay shook his head. "Fine. Say your bit."

"Thanks. This is the woman from Hawaii." It wasn't a question, so Seamus didn't respond. "So how I see it is, I might be tempted to view Kai as coming here instead of to the ranch as a lack of trust, but I could see it as her insecurity in what you had because of the distance of time that distorts things. It makes us see situations differently than they are. Did she know you were out of the Army? Did she expect your family to open their arms to her? I mean, it's been, what, nearly five years? Why come now? Maybe she wanted to be near you by being near your family, curiosity, or maybe she was in trouble. Regardless of the reason, she came from Hawaii to South Dakota, got a job, and waited. It counts for something. Something big."

"Maybe. But Kai is in trouble. I told her if she was ever in need to come here, even if I wasn't here, just come."

"Think that is why she's here?"

Seamus exhaled with aggression. "Hell, Stryker, she has a stalker, and she should have come to the ranch. What if he followed her?"

Stryker leaned forward on alert as though he could spot the transgressor in the room. "Fuck. How do you know?"

"The call I needed to make earlier? Her grandmother. She told me."

"Then she can't stay here, not in town."

"I can't kidnap her." Seamus rubbed the back of his neck and blew out a frustrated breath.

"No, but the girls can get her to come to the ranch."

"Make it happen because she isn't going to pull any more drunk assholes off her."

Seamus scraped his chair back loudly, but the effect was muted in the noisy room. He turned to Stryker and said, "And you did well as your girl's mouthpiece. Avery will be proud."

"Nah, what Avery told me to tell you is not to spank Kai. I just left that part out because I know you wouldn't think it was a good idea. You're the gentle brother."

Seamus nodded, then slapped his elder brother on the shoulder as he watched Kai peel off the third guy in almost as many minutes. Seamus stood up and knocked his chair over.

"You'd be surprised how itchy my palm is right now."

Seamus looked over his shoulder and told the guys, "Ride home together. My truck's bigger. Kai and I have a few things to discuss." Without a word, Declan tossed his keys to his brother, who slipped his set over to Stryker.

Stryker nodded. "And I bet your fingers have the urge to curl every time an asshole gets close to Kai. Believe me, I have become very familiar with both of those impulses."

Renee stared intensely at her big brother; her voice serious. "Shay, you're a big guy, in body and presence. You can be overwhelming, and I imagine that means you're that way in everything with Kai. Be careful not to crush her, even in your love."

He nodded. "Good advice."

SEAMUS HEADED TOWARD Kai's irritated voice and made it just as she shifted her hip out of the way of a patron who'd had too much to drink. The man was trying to shove some bills in her pants. Seamus grabbed her by the waist, pulling her smoothly behind him. He felt the grumble of irritation come from the center of his gut. He reached out to the man, casually grabbing his wrist, and squeezed.

"Stop, Seamus. You'll mess up my tips." Kai tried to separate Seamus' hand from the customer.

Seamus could see Kailani's face showing signs of relief and annoyance. So naughty. He hadn't noticed that before tonight, but he was seeing another side of his girl, and he both liked it and was concerned. Concerned for her skewed sense of safety for herself. His hand itched to set her straight. His baby girl, his sweetheart, his responsibility.

"Better than mess up all these pretty boy faces who want to be more than your patrons. Get your stuff, Kailani. You're coming with me."

The man who tried to slip his fingers into her pants complained. "Holy hell, Red Eagle, I'm just giving the girl a tip."

Shay snatched the money and tossed it on her tray. "Then put here, asshole, and quit trying to cop a feel."

The man gave Seamus a sheepish grin. "She's damn pretty."

"Yeah, and she's mine, so back off."

The partially inebriated man made a great show of raising his palms facing out and scooting back. "Hell, woman. You should have told me you were," he stopped to belch, "the property of Red Eagles. Come on, guys. Let's go to my place."

Seamus stepped closer to the man. "Should be a rule for everyone. Remember that."

All three men stumbled up from the table in an attempt to get their bearings. Seamus raised his hand to get Forrest's attention, but Carter intercepted the signal and nodded in his direction.

"I called Chauncey to come get them." Carter walked closer. "Be about three minutes. I'll keep watch and get them in the cab." Seamus tipped his chin in thanks.

When he turned back to Kai, she was gone. He searched the room and found her slipping into the back. If she thought that would stop him from following her, she had forgotten who he was.

He headed toward the same entrance she had gone through, his stride casual, his legs eating up the distance quickly. He didn't stop or hesitate but pushed through the door on the right like he owned the place. He did own a stake, but that was beside the point. Forrest didn't like anyone but employees in the back; once upon a time, Seamus respected that line. But now, the stakes were higher, and no barriers would stop him from getting to Kailani.

By the time he found her, she was cleaning the tray and shoving the tips in her pocket. He touched her shoulder, not quite knowing what her response would be, but preparing for a tongue-lashing. She turned and put the tray down to place her palms on his broad chest. Seamus remembered she'd once told him he looked good in everything she'd ever seen him wear, including his birthday suit. His cock swelled as he caught her eyes appraising him appreciatively. Was she reliving that same memory? His body ignited hotter as his recollections flooded back full of their skin-to-skin activities.

"You've got to stop following me, Seamus. I'm working."

"Kai, this isn't the place for you. Get your stuff. You're coming with me."

"Nope, I need to work." She had stepped back from him, and he wanted to grab her back into his arms.

"No, you don't." Her arms crossed to match her militant stare. She looked adorable. He'd laugh and kiss her if this wasn't so serious.

Seamus sighed heavily. "I'll get you a job on the ranch."

"As a paniolo?"

"Baby, I can't." He shook his head. "No, we have other things you can do. I'll not have you out with the livestock doing such a demanding and dangerous job. There is a lot more than herding cattle. There are fences to mend, hay to bring in, feed to move, and much more."

"Because you don't think I can?" Her injured pride was showing.

"Oh, I know you can do whatever you set your mind to, but I don't want you out there doing that work and getting hurt. There much better safer jobs for you, fulfilling jobs besides being a working cowboy."

"Nope, not happening."

"Kai, I said we would work it out. I'm serious about not staying here to put you in line to be manhandled. What kind of man would I be if I allowed that to happen under my nose?"

"Shay..." He loved it when she pleaded. It made him an asshole, he knew it, but he still loved it.

"Get your things now, baby, or we walk out of here without them, with you tossed over my shoulder and your ass on full display while I spank it."

She stomped her foot. Seamus grinned. "I remember why I was always irritated with you."

"Do you also remember who always won when it was important?" When the only response was her bow-shaped lips scrunched up, he nodded. "Good. Now stop. Go get your things, sweetheart. Daddy's serious."

"Oh!"

Chapter Seven

Seamus

Kai turned and stomped further to the back, where Seamus assumed her things were. He hailed Forrest, and the man walked closer.

"Taking my girl home, and she won't be back."

Forrest shook his head and laughed. "Guess I get enough business from your place to let you walk off with a server who was proving to be a good worker. She is definitely a good looker. You're a lucky man."

Shay groaned. "You too?"

His friend laughed again. "Have to be dead not to notice her, with that golden skin and long legs," he chuckled. "Sorry. Probably good you're taking possession before some others try. Don't mess it up, Red Eagle."

Seamus assessed his business partner for a moment, but when he sensed no genuine personal interest in Kai, but did everyone think they had a right to tell him how to run his life? And assume he was going to screw things up? Like you already did? Probably. Seamus gave a nod. "Appreciate it."

"Looks like you're losing your touch because she seems pretty irritated with you right now."

"Yep, right now, but after I remind her how good we are, it will change."

Forrest sobered. "Make sure you're extra good to her, Red Eagle. I get the impression she is dealing with something in her life."

Shay sobered. "Understood. Don't worry. The females we have added to the family won't allow anything else. Besides, my Mam would kick my ass across this continent and the next if I was anything but protective and sensitive to my girl's needs."

Forrest smiled. "I believe you're right. Have a good night, then. Night Kai. You always have a job here if you want it."

"You're firing me?"

Her eyes opened wide, and a mixture of disbelief and anger changed her exotic features into one gloriously pissed woman. She smacked Seamus' arm and seemed even angrier when he didn't flinch.

"No," Forrest pointed his thumb in Seamus' direction, "he did."

"And you let him?"

Her hands were propped on her hips, giving both men the look of death. Her incredulous tone brought a tiny smile that Forrest did well to hide.

"Sorry, little lady. He's a boss." Forrest gave Seamus a flustered look. "One that usually stays silent."

"Of course he is," she said disdainfully. "Everyone is afraid of the Red Eagles, or they run everything. Just my luck." But the heat in her words was less noticeable as her temper cooled.

Kai jerked away when Seamus tried to take her arm, walking ahead of him stiffly. Her movements showed that while she might not be irritated with Forrest, she still held Shay responsible for the outcome. He landed a substantial swat on her swaying, jeans-covered butt and smiled. He loved when Kai was sassy. Fucking loved it.

He watched her hand go to her ass, then threw him a glare full of contempt and something Shay couldn't quite decipher. Lust? His hand itched again, but knowing that his beautiful Kai had a plan and he had stormed in and changed it without warning, he gave her time to figure her reactions out. She was typically organized and didn't do things on the spur of the moment, so his taking control was doing a number on her processing.

Understanding that Seamus needed her even more than he had before leaving the islands would take time. Watching her cute as a button backside sway in front of him as she angrily headed for the entrance reminded Seamus of how much she meant to him. He didn't know how he'd been able to survive without her these last years, and Seamus sure as hell wasn't going to try now that he had her close. Time to get his head back in the game and stop existing... he intended on living again. Kailani attracted him in every way, but he realized he had to earn it. He owed her so much, beginning with an explanation and a job.

If that little firecracker even knew what he felt for her and how much he desperately needed her, she might run far and fast. Seamus realized he hadn't felt this alive since leaving Hawaii. Tonight, watching her ass jiggle as she stomped out of Cattleman's made him granite hard. Damn, he hadn't been this hard since the last time he gazed at her beauty. No matter the emotional state of Kailani, just her presence, the mere thought of her, sent his body into overdrive. He unlocked the truck and helped her inside, even though she jerked away the moment she was hoisted into the seat.

"Seamus, I can get in the vehicle myself."

"Kailani Aka, you know me and know that I believe a gentleman always helps a lady."

"You must have forgotten the rest of the things a gentleman does, like not leaving a lady hanging when she is waiting for you to contact her."

"You're absolutely right, and you have every reason to be angry with me. If you let me, I'll make it up to you."

"Yea, not sure you can or if I want you to. Just let it go. That was us before, not now."

He pulled her close. "It's now, too, if I have anything to do with it. Let it happen, Kailani."

She sniffed in obvious annoyance, but he also felt a softening in her. Granted, it was a slight softening, but that's all he needed for a foothold. He reached over to put on her seatbelt as she had loved him to do before, but now she slapped his hand away.

"Hell, woman. I'm just trying to do the things you like."

"Well, I don't like it anymore." She crossed her arms.

Seamus nodded in recognition of her emotional defense, but he intended to address her deception. His answer was casual and matter-of-fact.

"Yes, you do. Lying will get your ass paddled, so simmer down."

He closed the door and walked briskly over to the driver's side. He was in his seat, door closed, and reaching for his safety belt in a continuous fluid movement. He started his brother's truck and then pulled out.

After a few minutes, when they were on the long, empty road home, Seamus turned to take a fast glance at Kai, who was sitting with her arms crossed. She yawned. She looked exhausted.

"Where are you taking me? I have a motel room in town."

"Which one?"

"The Thunderbird."

He nodded but didn't respond. She watched him call someone and heard his brother Stryker answer.

"Hey, Kai is at the Thunderbird. Can the girls get her things from there?"

"Man, the Thunderbird... yeah, we gotcha covered. Room number?"

Seamus turned to Kailani to answer. She shook her head. "Just leave my things there. I don't need anyone to take over my life, Seamus."

Seamus answered Stryker. "Ask Joe or his wife."

"Done. We'll catch you back at the house."

"Thanks, bro."

Chapter Eight

Kailani

The brothers hung up, and an uncomfortable silence seemed to blanket the cab of the truck. Seamus took some time before he spoke again. That was okay with Kai because she was fuming that he was so high-handed. Kai couldn't believe she didn't see the depth of his manner sooner. She loved it in the bedroom, and when she wanted to feel protected, cherished by him, but this...

"I don't like what you just did, Seamus."

Seamus exited the road into what looked like a rest area without facilities. The truck was silent for a few moments, and just as Kai was going to fill it with words, Seamus spoke. His tone was low, edged with a darkness that felt ominous.

"Do you know what that motel specializes in?"

"Renting rooms?"

"Yeah, by the hour."

She swallowed. "Oh. But the owner and his wife were so nice."

"They are. Just usually, they don't get overnighters."

"But they won't let your brother or sister in my room." She shook her head. "Never mind. Red Eagles run this town, right?"

That seemed to anger him. "Of course not, but when Stryker explains you found us and are coming to the ranch, they'll be okay with that. Your room will be filled pretty soon."

She didn't want to admit it, but now that she knew what most used that motel for, kind as the owners were, she wouldn't have felt safe sleeping another night there.

"How long have you been in town?" he asked casually. It was too casual, his voice somber.

"A week."

"And at Cattleman's?"

"Five days. Are you really a boss there?"

"Technically. I'm part owner, but I don't have anything to do with day-to-day operations. That's Forrest. He owns the larger share. Didn't he tell you?"

Kai was silent again. "Kailani?"

"I didn't ask. Why would I?"

"I'm in charge of the day-to-day cattle operations at the ranch. I'm the final boss there and am responsible for the hands and the working ranch employees, and as such, I can't allow you to do dangerous work."

He held up his hand automatically. "My sister grew up here and can be as hard as nails, but she isn't allowed to do the work of a paniolo. My father won't allow it, nor will anyone else on the ranch. So save your breath." He ran his hand through his hair, leaving it adorably spikey. "We protect those we care about. For me, that includes you. I imagine it will translate to all the men in our family, but the trade-off is you get the women to champion you."

"You don't even know me now. I could have changed."

"True, and you don't know me, but I won't ever allow you to be in harm's way if I can help it. And you're here, so I plan on us getting to know each other again."

Kai ignored his last remark and admired his hair, left uncut for her. It was a powerful message. "If I can't work to earn my way, why are you taking me to the ranch?"

"I invited you, and I meant it then, and I mean it now. I claimed you a long time ago. I will always want you here, with me. The better question is, after all this time, why are you here, Kailani? I was told several years ago that you were engaged. When I heard nothing, and you never answered my calls, I assumed you were married."

She gasped. "Is that why?"

"Why?"

"Why did you never come back for me?"

"It was part of the reason. The first part was I was severely injured during the first mission back in the field, and I didn't want you to feel obligated to be with me if I wasn't going to heal completely. I thought I had to be a whole man for you. I know that was wrong, but I would never saddle you with less than who you knew before."

"How could you think that about me?" Kai was hurt at the thought of him not believing in her love for him.

"I wanted everything to be the same as it was. I've learned a lot since that time, and my family taught me that being alive in any state was better than being dead."

"Newsflash, they were right."

He flashed her a grin. "I know. That's when I called a buddy of mine when I couldn't get hold of you. Why didn't you call me?"

Kai answered hesitantly. "I had a little trouble with someone, so I changed my number. He had the old number, and I blocked him, but it didn't matter. He would call from all sorts of numbers. So I changed numbers."

"Why didn't you call and tell me?"

"I didn't want you to think I was helpless or pretending to get your attention after you went radio silent for so long. I didn't trust you any longer."

The cab was still except for the rhythmic sound of Seamus' hand rubbing up and down Kailani's thigh. He started the truck again, merging onto the road again. Finally, they turned down an avenue into even thicker darkness.

"No street lights?"

Seamus smiled. He had turned on his hi-beams a while ago, but now he added the big guns, the cab spotlights. She looked over at him with a question on her lips, but Seamus, being Seamus, anticipated her confusion and answered her unspoken query.

"Running lights on the sides and a light bar on top. We all have them. We drive a lot of dark roads, and it's dangerous not having light to see the road or what might be in it."

"Yes, that's smart."

After a few more miles of silence, Seamus spoke again. "I learned just tonight, when I spoke to your Nan, that you never were engaged. She also told me that you were on your way here. She neglected to tell me you left a week ago."

Kai softened. "You spoke to Nan tonight?"

"I did. I wanted to try you one last time. I don't know why I picked today after so long, but I did. When you didn't answer, I tried the house again, and I'm grateful it worked. Your grandmother is worried about you, Kai."

"I know."

"She told me to take care of you and about some guy who thought you were together as a couple. Something about your family land. She called him a silly boy. I do like your Nan."

Kai sighed. "It's true. I thought I might come here, far from where he would think I'd go. I'm not sure why but I hoped it would be a safe place if I needed one."

"It is. The only big problem with that plan was you never called so we could bring you home. We'll talk about this tomorrow, but your grandmother said not to let you go home until she said it was safe."

"For a woman who rarely speaks to people she doesn't know, she sure talked a lot with you."

He grinned in the darkened cab. "I have charm. Besides, your Nan knows me. I've met her several times, remember?"

"You have something, alright, and that was a while ago. Your confidence hasn't waned."

Kai allowed a small smile to tilt her lip. The first since she'd seen Seamus tonight. She could feel her body relax into being with him again. Not that she would give up any of her emotional ground but just knowing he would take care of her demons felt good. It shouldn't, Kai told herself, but it did.

Kai didn't know what else to say. Seamus hadn't forgotten her or their connection. It bothered her that he thought she was engaged and probably married. They had both hurt these last years, and she wasn't sure they could recover from the separation but what she did know is her attraction to this man was more potent than ever.

He'd protected her tonight as he had at the beach in Hawaii with the pickpocket. He was angry she had put herself in harm's way tonight, just like then. And the thing about her Seamus, he didn't hold a grudge. He took care of the problem and moved on.

Kai didn't know what would happen between them, but her panties were already steamy, and that long-ago sensation of the tingle of attraction had her wiggling in her seat. Seamus quickly looked at her before returning his eyes to the road. He smiled before continuing to speak.

"Horses."

"What?" asked Kai.

"How good are you with horses?"

Seamus tried to rein in his rioting emotions. Lock it down, Red Eagle. She was incredible. Kai was still everything he wanted.

"Great, why?" She turned to him; her curiosity peaked.

He nodded. "Can you work with them?"

"Yeah, I can. I love horses."

"Okay then. You can work with the horses."

After another few moments of silence, Kai asked. "Is that much of a job? I mean, how many can you have?"

"Last count? A hundred and fourteen."

"A hundred and..." Kai was silent again. Then she asked, "Why?"

"Working dude ranch, remember? Think you'd like to take care of the pregnant mares and the foals? We have about fifteen right now. More coming."

"Really? I'd love it."

Seamus gave her a slight smile. "Good. That's done then."

"How much are you paying?"

"How much am I... okay, that's a good question. I'll ask Stryker and Renee. That's their job."

She nodded as a slow smile crossed her lips, then it was quickly gone. "Okay."

"Well, alright then. We won't talk about it tonight, but tomorrow we'll hash out this whole clusterfuck you seem to have gotten yourself into."

"I didn't get myself into anything," she said vehemently.

"Sorry, that sounded judgmental, and that isn't how I meant it. Look, we've had a full night. Things will start coming out wrong if we continue on a serious note. Can we pend the important stuff until after we get some sleep?"

"Okay."

He reached his hand over and squeezed her thigh. That got her tingling in all the tender places again. He drove into an area he identified as the family parking area. In the dark, it appeared to be made of bare earth instead of asphalt and situated on the side of the enormous house.

The truck was switched off, and the lights left on. Seamus turned to her and slid his hand curled comfortingly around the back of her neck, drawing her to him carefully. Kai could have pulled away, but she wanted this kiss as much as he did. His lips descended slowly to give her time to stop him, but she could do nothing but lean into him. The connection of flesh, after so long, nearly overwhelmed Kai.

Her hands sought his hair, and the length vaguely registered again before she leaned further in, opening to his exploration. The console bit into her hip as she edged closer to his reacquaintance with her mouth, and her moan didn't seem to have an end. His answering groan was fuel to her internal fire. Her need for him surpassed what it ever was during their time in Hawaii, something she didn't even know was possible.

More lights. Seamus slowly pulled away, placing one final kiss before raising his head. A slow, easy grin spread across his face.

"Mmm, I've missed your perfection, sweetheart. But I should spank your perky ass for letting those randy cowboys manhandle you."

"It was fine, Seamus. I can handle myself. I've been doing it for years."

"And I should kick my own ass for making that a necessity. You won't have any of that happen to you again. I'm your protection now. And that also means you won't put yourself in harm's way again. You're my sweet baby girl, and I won't let anyone bother you."

Her core tingled, and her hips wiggled at the sensation in response to his words. She was his. He had no idea how inadequate that was in describing how she felt about Seamus. His very presence drew her in, and there was no doubt that she was doomed. So doomed.

Chapter Nine

Kailani

Kai caught the flash of porch light in her peripheral vision. Seamus grumbled.

"The only way anyone could have beat us home is if they left right after we did."

Kai had to agree. They had stopped, sure. Then they'd driven slowly to get some essential talking done, but they couldn't have taken that much time.

"Come on, baby girl, let's get you inside and in the tub for a good soak. You look dead on your feet."

Kia felt that earlier tightening in her chest when Seamus discovered she was being touched, no, manhandled, by the drunken sods that night. They were very polite, handsy drunks, but it was still difficult to deal with. She had worried that he would really hurt someone. He was tense, demanding, and protective. Possessive. Just like now. Her belly clenched when his hand went to the back of her neck. He held her to his gaze, leaning down to place his forehead against hers.

"You good, baby?"

All she could do was nod. She wanted Shay with every molecule of her being, and she melted when he sealed his lips to hers. This man. Why did she ever think she could live without him? His gentle touch and manner made up for any take-charge behavior that occasionally reared its head. Her lover, her daddy when she needed him to take care of her, her man.

"I've got you, always, baby. Hold tight while I come around."

Seamus got out to walk around and open Kai's door when it was whipped open by Saoirse Renee. A dog appeared from the darkness, and he seemed to try to push Renee from the doorway.

"Maverick, back away. You too, Renee." The dog listened but not Renee.

Maverick went to Seamus' side as if escorting him around the truck. The dog seemed to know Seamus would allow him to follow but not lead. The dog had instincts. Seamus rubbed his head for a few seconds before he walked the last couple of steps to the truck door.

"We'll feed you if you're hungry and make up a bed for you." Renee seemed to want to take charge, but she was also cautiously standing in his way.

"Oh, I don't want to put you out." Kai was a little out of her depth.

"Shay, tell her it's okay. We have plenty of spare rooms."

"Renee."

Seamus said his sister's name in an elongated, you're overstepping, kind of way. "Pushy much?" He turned back to Kai. "She's right, though. But if you want to sleep in my room with me, you can."

"I don't want to put anyone out. I mean, I can sleep on a couch or something."

Seamus snaked his arm around her waist. "Sleeping with me will put people out the least."

"Shay, stop telling her that so you can get her in your bed."

He shrugged. "Okay, how about I put you next to me, and you can be close but not too close. For tonight."

"Thank you, that would be nice."

Avery, who had come out with Renee, headed back up the steps to the front door. "I'm warming up leftovers and adding some dessert. Would you like some, Kai?"

"Don't worry about me," said Kailani after a slight hesitation. Her belly was quietly rumbling.

Teagan seemed to read that pause accurately. "We took a quicker route and wanted you as comfortable as possible, as quickly as we could. We called ahead, and her key was out for us. We would have taken longer, but Kai is evidently immaculate."

Seamus grunted. Kai hadn't noticed how much he did that. "A shortcut that you were not to take at night. I'll be discussing this with the guys when they get here."

"Spoilsport, but they already know. They beat you home too. They said it was like she was packed to run at any moment." Renee's unasked question hung in the air. It was ignored. "Where did you go, anyway? Strike that question. We just wanted to be here to help pave the way for Kai. So, hungry?" asked Renee.

Teagan answered for her. "Of course you're hungry. How could you not be? You worked your butt off at Cattleman's."

"Oh, but really, I..." Kai's attempt to refuse was thankfully ignored.

A familiar deep voice sounded in Kai's ear as he pushed Renee out of the truck doorway. "Accept the offer, baby. I know you didn't get a dinner break."

Kailani nodded and sighed. That man was already reading her mind, as he had in Hawaii. He was anticipating her responses, and Lord help him if the man began making her choices for her. That was over the line, and she'd tell him so, but it felt so good to have him take care of her in the meantime. She'd missed that about being with Seamus and wanted it again, just for the time she would be here. She hoped it was a while.

"Thank you. I didn't eat dinner tonight because I was running late. Then we were so busy I didn't stop to grab food because I didn't get a break. I had no idea there would be so many people there."

Avery and Teagan made tsking sounds and murmured about working on an empty stomach.

Avery said, "You're here with us now. The Red Eagles take care of their own. You're Seamus' lady, so you're family."

Renee nodded. "Seamus made a good investment in that place, but I don't think he meant that any of us should work there. Not permanently, anyway. I'm headed up. Wanna follow me, Kai? The guys already packed your stuff into your room. You didn't bring very much. You travel light." Again, that unspoken query, Kai chose not to respond.

"I'll help Avery while Renee gets the bed made," said Teagan.

"I'll check on the bunkhouses," said Callen. "Save me some pie."

Seamus reached over and kissed Kai before she made it to the stairs leading to the upper level. It was fast but thorough, leaving no doubt in anyone's mind, hers included, that he was claiming Kailani. Kai wanted to call him on it, but then she'd have to challenge how she responded to his touch, which was not what she wanted to do right now. It felt too good.

Carter said he'd head to the furthest livestock barn. Stryker and Declan headed for the closer one. And that seemed to be that. Everyone knew their place and the jobs that were expected of them. They were a diverse family, but they seemed to have lives that interwove and flowed with little resistance. Like hers once did.

Her Nan and grandfather had such a life. A life of purpose and meaning, bound with others. They were a constant force in Kai's life, and she was attracted to that way of connecting, that peace. She was drawn to Seamus' family's way of life. But things might look very different in the morning, she reminded herself. Time to clean the night's grime and weariness off, then she would eat and sleep. Tomorrow would bring what it brought.

Seamus

Seamus jumped in the shower. The goal was to have a quick, thorough wash, but he could smell a soft, lingering scent that could only be Kailani's. She had that delicate, heady fragrance of plumeria that wafted through the air as she passed. This is the shower she would have used to bathe. It connected their rooms. Seamus' parents loved the Jack and Jill bathrooms, so one was between each pair of bedrooms upstairs.

As her scent brought Kailani to mind, Seamus thought of her soft skin, sassy attitude, and acceptance of his protection for now. That trust she was placing in him to keep her safe combined with the rest, and he ached for her. His muscles tightened in need, and his cock responded by turning into a pillar of granite. He slid his soapy hand down and rubbed his member as he thought of her sweet lips on his, how she tasted, and the fire that burned when he touched her. He pulled roughly on his cock when he recalled her skin on his before leaving Hawaii and what she would feel like now as he filled her with his need, and she milked his yearning from him.

Suddenly, ribbons of ecstasy shot against the shower wall, and his relief was immediate, his satisfaction the best since leaving his Hawaiian beauty and yet, in the same breath, woefully inadequate. He wanted to sate his need inside his girl. That was his new goal in addition to ensuring she was safe from this Rufus Paolo guy. And that sent his thoughts in another direction. He would have more maintenance showers until he could get Kai in his bed again.

Kai and her Nan scoffed at his concern over the man, but in Seamus' experience, unrequited love could be a problem, a big problem. He would never underestimate the power of desire. He'd seen usually rational men do irrational things in the name of unrequited love. If the goal was a greedy one, there were no bounds. He finished his shower and toweled off, wrapping it around his waist just as the door from Kai's bedroom opened.

"Seamus..."

Her shocked expression gave way to appreciation and, if he was reading her right, hunger for something other than food for the stomach. He'd be a fool not to capitalize on it just a little.

"Hey, come in. I'm almost done and decent." His hand waved in the direction of his towel.

Kai's head followed where his hand indicated, and he'd be damned if she didn't start to lick her lips but stopped herself from completing the act. He perused her long, slender legs, brown and unblemished. Could he get any stiffer? Evidently, he could. He was so full his cock was almost painful as though he hadn't just relieved his need in the shower. In response, Seamus could feel the throbbing pulse of rushing blood and expected to feel light-headed at any moment. Now he felt like he carried a cement rod between his legs.

He grabbed himself and squeezed, trying to relieve the strain, but that only made him worse. The joke was on him. He should have known he was playing with fire.

"Hey," said Kai with a slight hint of a grin.

"Hey."

"Whatcha got there?" she teased.

Turning toward Kai, he huffed a laugh. "I don't want to shock you, but I'm so aroused right now, I'm afraid I'll burst. You do this to me with a simple whiff of your perfume or the mere thought of you in the same house. Kailani Aka, I missed you."

"Seems you really missed me. I missed you too, Seamus. It's as though we were never apart." She blushed. "Well, except I'm more independent and older. Oh, and we aren't sleeping in the same bed."

"And you're wiser, more beautiful, more impressive. Sassier." He grinned. "I like the feisty you. And we could sleep in the same bed if you wanted to."

"I'm more opinionated out of necessity. I have more confidence and..." She shook her head. "Tomorrow we'll talk... about everything." She nodded at his cock. "Want me to help you with that problem tonight?"

"Yes, on the help, but not going to let you. We need to take a little time and reacquaint ourselves with us of yesterday and blend that couple into the us of today. But be warned, my girl, when I claim you this time, it will be for all time. And I won't wait long." His severe tone was full of warning. The assurance of his intense need to have her was just as potent. "When the time comes, I'll remember to lock the door behind us, but I can't promise to be able to restrain myself from tasting your succulent body." He turned on his warrior Viking look. "Now get out of here, Kailani, before I forget I'm trying to be a gentleman."

Seamus pinched her butt cheek as she turned. Her squeal and outraged expression when she looked back at him brought a devious smile to his face. If he had his way, he'd be doing much more than pinching that fit bottom. She was thawing, and he would go slow if it killed him. He hoped it didn't.

Chapter Ten

*K**ailani***
The morning was bright, heralding breakfast that was noisy in a familiar way. Plates and bowls were drawn across the wooden slab table, created from a monstrosity of an oak tree. Utensils were scraping the sides of serving dishes, accompanied by chairs being dragged across solid oak flooring, mellowed by age. Kailani looked around the room and was impressed with the activity that wasn't chaos.

Seamus was already seated when she entered the room, but as the men saw her, every single male made motions to stand, but when they saw Seamus was already on his feet, they all reseated. Wow, that was embarrassing. She didn't require or desire that kind of attention. Kai understood it was manners but hadn't seen it in action too often with her peers.

"Sit here, baby. Do you want coffee or tea? Juice?" Seamus waved at a clean plate at the spot next to him. "Help yourself to breakfast. It will be a full morning around here, but you should get oriented to the ranch today. There will be time enough to learn what we do in the yearling stable. We'd like to add a nursery corner.

"I've told everyone you'll be able to monitor the mares and foals as well as gentle the yearlings. We all know they respond better to a woman's touch, and that's important when we want to break them for riding. The girls enjoy them, but they have their own jobs, so having someone there all the time will be great."

Carter nodded. "If you're going to be in there permanently, then I don't mind putting my pregnant mares there as well. It isn't ideal right now, as I've kept them with me in a pen near where I keep healing horses. Those on the mend are unpredictable, so I corral them mostly because I don't want them to take off and reinjure themselves. Pregnant mares ready to foal are vulnerable and pretty skittish. I think the yearling stable has a good setup, but if you need anything, let me know. I'll take care of it."

"Thank you, Carter." It seems the men were setting her up without any disruption to their day. She admired their ability to adjust enough to include time to integrate a new person.

He nodded, then turned to the others at the table, "I'm heading out. Won't be back for lunch, but I'll catch up at dinner. I've got to train a few of the new hires on the trail ride route. I'll keep my satellite phone on me and my locator."

Carter, who wasn't a Red Eagle, but a family member by choice, worked with Seamus to oversee the running of the ranch's livestock. As she understood it, Carter was Stryker's best friend, participating in family activities since childhood. As she watched him, Kai suspected there was something else under his teasing of Renee, but she could be wrong.

"Hey, sweetheart, I've got some things I need to take care of this morning, so if you want to, check out the house and the surrounding areas, maybe call your Nan. We can meet back here at lunch. Then I'll get you to the stables and start orienting you to things. I never asked, but do you need to get clothes for working the horses? Servers don't wear the same kind of boots as you'll need."

Before Kailani could reply, Avery said, "That's perfect. We have some paperwork for Kai before she starts, and I think Renee and I were going to take her to the lodge, so we'll just add a run to town, as well. We'll be back by lunch, and we can then hand her over to Seamus."

Teagan, who seemed to be the quiet one of the group, said, "I've got some work to do for the lodge, so I'll just go do it in the office and will go over when you all go. So glad it's Saturday, and I don't have classes."

"So long as you remember that we have plans for this evening, Miss Manz," said Declan with a twinkle in his eye.

"Dec, it isn't going to take all day."

"Just don't make us late." Did all the Red Eagle men have that panty-scorching tone? Damn.

Teagan kissed him quickly. "I wouldn't do that."

Declan laughed and slapped Stryker on the back. "Looks like you won't get much help this morning anyway."

Stryker grunted. "In case you ladies didn't notice, you have talked around Kailani but not invited her into the conversation. She does have a voice and an opinion."

Stryker looked over at Kai and raised his eyebrow to encourage her to speak. Kai didn't quite get the message. Callen leaned down and smiled at Kai.

"I imagine this is all a bit overwhelming with so many people taking charge of your life. And you just thought it would only be Seamus you had to worry about." He winked and nodded in Stryker's direction. "He's opening the door for you to say what you want. You have to be careful with us Red Eagles. We tend to take over when given the slightest chance."

"Hey, that's my girl you're too close to, little brother," said Seamus as he reentered the dining room from the kitchen with a fresh cup of coffee. The message was clear, keep away from what's mine.

"I'm simply encouraging Kai not to let the girls railroad her into doing things."

Seamus shouldered into the mix and kissed her cheek. "He's right. Give them an inch, and they'll take a country mile."

"I'm sure he's talking about all the Red Eagles." Renee turned to Kai. "If you don't want to go," started Renee, "then—"

Kai stood. "I'll fill out paperwork, visit your lodge, grab what I need for working and come back here for lunch, and go with you, Seamus, afterward. But, just for a little information on me, I only have two brothers who are a few years older than me, so this packed room is a little overwhelming. I'm used to running my own day and speaking my mind, but I find it works better if everyone says their piece and I speak at the end. So, are we all good? Schedule created?"

The room was silent for a long minute. Kai could almost hear the wheels churning in each person's head. She waited. She could calm children, horses, and upset guests, so she could manage this lot. Stryker's family meant well, but they were a little out of control. Too many words to say or what they thought needed to be said.

Seamus leaned down and planted a kiss that promised so many things later. "That's my girl."

Kai turned to face Seamus. This man, who did so many delicious things to her by just walking into the room, met her stare with laughing eyes.

"The jury is still out on our status," she said.

Seamus never wavered. "No, it isn't. You're just being stubborn. And we still have that conversation this afternoon about everything else." He kissed her again, clearly confident that he was in control. "Have a good morning, sweetheart."

Seamus stood and turned toward Callen, "Let's get going, Cal. I have to check out your new people this morning to fit them with horses."

Callen scraped back his chair, shoving the last of his toast in his mouth, and joined Seamus, both donning hats and boots, before heading out the door.

"That's my cue," said Stryker. "Avery, I have a business meeting this afternoon, but they called and asked if I'd meet them in town for lunch. You get Kai squared away and we'll connect afterward." He leaned down to kiss his girl.

"Come on, Kai. We have things to do, too," said Renee. "You'll want to start Monday, but that won't happen until we get the formalities taken care of. Stryker is a stickler for paperwork."

Avery murmured. "Among other things."

Stryker swung his hand to make contact with his sister's butt, but she sidestepped him quickly, an obviously practiced move, and Kai smiled. She was surprised when he redirected his swing to land on Avery's ass.

"Ouch, Stryker. I'm still... just ouch." She turned a little pink.

"Sorry, baby. I got carried away."

"Whatever."

Avery turned even redder. They must all be a little like Seamus with the spanking bug. These were people you could count on. This bunch was crazy and loving, and she yearned to be a part of them. They reminded Kailani of her own family in their closeness. Thinking of her family gave her an unexpected longing to call Nan. Now, if she could share her information with Seamus later today without him coming unglued, she'd do okay here.

The morning went well. Paperwork wasn't something Kai loved to do, but she could get through it. Having Avery, who appeared to be Stryker's office everything, and Renee, who handled payroll, personnel issues, and her brothers, plying her with coffee, then tea, it was a leisurely morning. Forms complete, they had a rushed trip to the small town. Kai was afraid that she wouldn't be able to find what she needed, but it seemed calf-high work boots, jeans, and cowboy hats were something everyone considered required attire.

There was a surprisingly decent assortment to choose from. She grabbed three pairs of jeans to add to the two worn ones she'd brought for comfort. Kai added a handful of sturdy shirts that still let her look like a woman, which was a personal must with Seamus. She decided to go with two long-sleeved button-downs too. Finally, she picked a chestnut-colored leather hat and boots that came awfully close to matching.

The last hour before lunch found them wandering through the lodge, the love child of Avery and Renee. It was beautiful, and the activities offered in the community nearby were a great alternative to dude ranching.

The concept was that vacationing family members not interested in being what the ladies described as "duders" could enjoy lodge life for a week. Who wouldn't want a week of hot springs, hot tubs, swimming, shopping, excellent meals, spa experiences, and in the winter, skiing, snowboarding, and other sports?

It was much like her family's big island adventures but South Dakota style. The part of the ranch that Kai was most attracted to was the equines. She loved horses, had grown up with them, and had worked and trained with them as a vital part of their family ranching business. But she wasn't given the job of taking care of anything but reservations at their ranch. Here she was going to be given a chance to spread her wings, be a part of the working ranch, and she loved Seamus for allowing that to happen. Not quite a paniolo, but close enough.

Feelings of her deep affection for how Seamus took care of her flowed warm and cozy through her, causing that familiar but little-experienced tingle to release wetness in the gusset of her panties. She grew slippery with her growing arousal. Seamus would like to know that he did that to her.

Kai knew Seamus, as confident as he appeared, wanted the assurance that he could rekindle these types of responses in her. He might say he had no doubt of their deep connection but was it even possible after so long? She questioned her own attraction. Was it desire or familiarity and the knowledge that this man would protect her at all costs? She hoped it was desire and understanding.

"Lunch is here every day, six days a week. On Sunday, we fend for ourselves," said Carter as he took a big spoonful of the stew.

"Okay," said Kai, "but I'm not family. It looks like the rest of the workers eat in the bunkhouse."

The room was quiet except for the crunching of a cracker. Kai looked around and saw all eyes were on Seamus. Declan spoke. "Looks like your question, Shay."

Seamus seemed flustered, and that amused her. Her big, bad Army pilot, who ran a vast working ranch, had trouble answering a question. Yes, that was funny, but Kai carefully swallowed her merriment. She met his stare with one as innocent as possible. He sighed.

"First, because you're the only woman employed on the working part of the ranch to handle livestock, there's no way you're going to sit with a bunch of guys who would rather share your bed than share a meal."

The women all frowned at him. Kai nodded. "Okay, that was kinda harsh, but what about sleeping? I can bed down in the stables."

"Kailani, darlin', tread carefully." Shay's tone was deceptively calm. "Pushing the limits is all fun and games until you step over the line." Seamus was holding her stare. The communication was loud and clear. "I give all my employees a real bed to sleep on. And again, you aren't sleeping in with the men. That would be a criminal act."

"I can handle myself." The conversation was becoming a battle of wills, and Kai knew it was infantile, but she felt driven to continue.

Seamus snorted. "I know you think you can, and in most cases, I would agree, but in the face of part-timers or seasonal workers, safety isn't guaranteed. I'd like to vouch for them, but I can't. Not where women are concerned because I just don't know. For you, for any female, the answer will always be no."

"But there has to be a better way. I don't understand how you expect me to stay here and work if you can't see your way to provide an appropriate space for me. This wasn't a good idea."

"You're my girl, Kailani, so you aren't going to sleep anywhere I don't put you."

"I'm not sure that's a strong enough reason when your other workers are not here. Not even Carter stays in the house."

Declan added quietly. "We gave him his own place as a privilege, Kai, not a separation. Carter is part of us. So are you, now."

Kai turned to stare at Declan, who shrugged as if the reality of his statement was untouchable.

"Technically," continued Seamus, "you've been part of us since I claimed you before leaving Hawaii. Because I'm the boss, and I said so is enough reason. You're staying in the house. Eating, sleeping, and whatever else you need to do will be done here. And Carter has a cabin, so he doesn't stay here... by choice. His."

"Bossy much?" taunted Kai.

"Kailani, that's it. We aren't discussing this further."

She sighed loudly. "But Shay, won't that make the others think I'm being given preferential treatment? It could cause bad blood between us."

"Kai, let it go," Renee whispered.

"But I don't want to cause trouble," she responded.

"You won't," said Callen reaching for a piece of cornbread.

Kai put her paper napkin on the table and rose to stand. "Maybe I should just go back to town and Cattleman's."

"Dammit, Kailani, you're my girl, which means you're staying in the house with me. I'll let you have your own room but not outside this house. Now sit down and finish lunch. We have a full afternoon."

Kai sat heavily back into her chair. The room was still quiet except for spoons clanging against ceramic bowls. Finishing his bowl of stew quickly, Seamus stood and grabbed his lunch dishes.

"Come to the horse barn when you're done eating. Finish your food before you come out because I need your full attention on what we're doing, and being hungry distracts a person." Then Seamus strode to the kitchen.

"No news there, but I think he didn't want to announce it like that," said Avery.

Renee shook her head. "He has done nothing but announce it last night and this morning. He's sure into you, Kai. Was he that possessive in Hawaii?"

"In the beginning."

Avery cocked her head. "Then what happened?"

"It got worse."

The women laughed.

Carter got up and waved to the girls remaining at the table. "I might be a little late for dinner. Don't wait but save me some." He ran his finger down Renee's cheek and strode toward Seamus' direction, boot heels scuffing the old wood floors. The kitchen screen slammed shut a few seconds later.

"Don't play with Shay's affections." Renee pierced her with a sharp look. "He might be a troublesome brother sometimes, but he has a big heart, and I love him. So if you plan to leave him, do it now."

"Stop it. Can't you tell she's in love with him?" asked Teagan sharply.

Kailani let the tears she'd held over the reasons she'd left Hawaii, the disconnect and reconnect with Seamus, and her fear that her life would never be her own, fall. The messages she was receiving were mixed and confusing. She had no idea about the sensitivity of her partially mended heart. She brushed them away roughly. Maybe coming here wasn't the best idea.

Avery leaned over and patted her on the back. "Hey, Seamus just declared he claimed you again. Renee can be a little harsh in her protection of the guys. Do you have feelings for Seamus because he has never been this way with anyone else. He's such a gentle soul."

"I have so many feelings, they're overwhelming. I always have, but things have changed. He's changed. How does he know he still wants me?"

Avery smiled. "I don't think that's the problem. The real problem is to make him play his hand, not keep it close to his chest. He wants to let himself go and take you in completely, but he has to reconcile things. Like your desires for him. Stryker says he has to deal with his demons before he can fully commit, to you, to anyone."

Renee nodded. "Sorry I came on strong. It's just that Seamus is our gentle giant around here. Stryker takes care of everyone, but he doesn't mess with your place on the ranch unless you're family. Seamus does. If they work on the ranch, he watches over them. And if you're family, he is demanding but protective. I imagine he's also possessive and damn bossy if you're his woman."

Teagan stood from the end of the table where she had been sitting. "It looks like you have a few things to take care of yourself before you're available to take this romance between you further. So I recommend bringing Seamus in on your problems, and he will begin to open up about his. By the way, any idea why he hasn't cut his hair?"

"I do. But that's Seamus' story to tell. Thanks, ladies." Kailani's phone dinged with an incoming message. "Looks like the gentle giant is impatient. Gotta go. See you at dinner."

Kai wasn't sure about forever yet, but she did want to explore it and the reason behind Seamus' hot and cold behavior toward her. She figured Renee and

Avery were right. His last military mission had something to do with the recovery difficulties afterward. Seamus had alluded to some things, but she was reasonably sure that wasn't the whole story.

If Kai was going to see if they were truly meant for each other, like she once thought they were, then she would have to pay attention. She'd take every opportunity to slip under his defenses while trying not to let her own wall completely slip away. Shay would become the warrior Viking everyone jokingly nicknamed him to resolve her Rufus problem. She knew he would protect her at all costs.

Maybe Teagan was right; opening up was the best first step. She would tell him just enough to encourage his sharing. Kai hoped it would be enough because she could quickly lose herself in this man.

Chapter Eleven

S eamus

Three weeks had passed since Seamus brought Kailani home, and he'd tried to get her to share more about the trouble her Nan had alluded to, but Kai wouldn't elaborate. She'd simply said he knew it all; namely, Paolo was a jerk, and she needed to get away from his manipulation and near stalking-like behaviors. Kai insisted there was nothing else. Except, there must be, because why else would she have decided to show up here after four years of opportunity?

Still bugged that the guy Seamus had considered his buddy had given him false information, he'd called Frank Cassini.

"Hey, Red Eagle! How the hell are you?"

"Frank. Good, I'm good. How's the family?"

The man hesitated and then replied with a sad note to his words. "She left me about a year ago."

"Shit, man, sorry about that."

Thankfully, Seamus and Kailani were reconnecting. Seamus had an idea he knew some of the reasons. The dude had proven himself untrustworthy, but he did have an idea of how hard that was on a person to lose a loved one. He had high hopes for a forever in their future.

The two men shot the breeze for a few moments, and then Seamus asked, "Hey, remember the woman I asked you about? Kailani Aka?"

"Oh, yeah. The girl who got married to Rufus. Well, I'd assume she got married after being engaged for so long but, come to think of it, I never got an invitation to the wedding."

"Rufus?" Seamus thought playing dumb was the best route.

"Paolo. See, he's a cousin... on my mother's side."

"How can that be? Are you Hawaiian?"

"No, that's the crazy thing. Rufus' father, Clifton, is my mother's half-brother. Her father had a family before hers, and they were in Hawaii. So, that's why I should have gotten an invitation."

"Is it Rufus who told you he was engaged to Kailani?"

"Yeah. Kind of a crazy guy, though. Not sure marrying a looker like that Kailani girl was in her best interest. But, not my business what turns people on, right? Hey, what's this about? Did something happen to your friend?"

Seamus stiffened and wanted to go right through the phone to teach Cassini that you don't leave a woman to be with a man that you might be worried about treating her right. The fact that it was Seamus' girl made it unacceptable and intolerable. His voice turned to marble. Cold and hard.

"Why would you ask that?" Seamus asked.

Now, Cassini changed his tone. He began a swift back peddling. "Ah, no reason. I'm talking out my ass. I don't know what they're doing now."

"If you suspected or knew this Paolo guy wasn't good with women, you should have warned Kailani and any other women he was with of his behaviors."

"Look, Seamus, I don't know anything. There were just some rumors in the family, man. Honest. I had no proof he was anything but a gentleman."

"Yeah, well, let me tell you that Rufus Paolo was never engaged to Ms. Aka, nor was he even her boyfriend. He is, however, stalking her. You better put the fear of a combat veteran in him before he finds out just what can happen when you intimidate and bother with women after they tell you they aren't interested."

Cassini became a little belligerent. "Wait now, Red Eagle, you don't know that."

"I do. Kailani Aka is mine. She and her family have told me that Rufus Paolo won't leave her alone. So, if you like your cousin, or even if you don't, I'd advise you to tell him to leave her alone. I will protect her at all costs."

"I'll tell him, but where are you? I heard you got out of the Navy."

"Whether I'm in or out doesn't matter. I have plenty of buddies, and you know their skill level. So, just share the good advice, and we'll all live our best lives. Sorry about your family. Hope things get better for you."

The man grunted back, and Seamus hung up. His anger was still pretty white hot. What the hell did Cassini think when the rumors were Paolo was dangerous with women or even could be? Cassini was an armed forces member and should be protecting people, not turning a blind eye.

Seamus knew if he were back in Hawaii, he'd probably end up in jail. While Shay wanted satisfaction, he was glad there was too much of a distance between them and that his girl had the protection of his family. He didn't trust Cassini not to figure out where Seamus was and tell his cousin. Then all hell would break loose. Yeah, he shouldn't have called. Time to figure out a plan for keeping his girl safe. Without her catching on to what he was doing.

Seamus was relieved that Kailani didn't force him to make an edict. She stayed in the house without pushing that envelope. He guessed he could have allowed her to have the hospitality manager's little room in the lodge since he didn't use it, but Seamus didn't want that. Thankfully, Kai had stayed in the house, in the room next to his. If he had allowed her to move into the cottage, Seamus would have had to change his agreement after the phone call. Now he didn't have to mention it.

Shay knew he was confusing her. Some days he was moody and stayed away; other days, he treated her like his lover, and they were a committed couple. Neither were accurate representations of his feelings or facts. Seamus wanted them together in every way, and that was the goal he was working, ineffectually, toward. Maybe he should talk to his brothers, Stryker, and Declan. Get some insight on this claiming a partner thing.

His Kai was a woman to be reckoned with when it came to tasks. If she felt it was a challenge she could meet, and a couple he didn't think she should try to meet, that sassy woman knuckled down and pushed through. There was an overwhelming urge to spank that firm, rounded backside that swayed as she walked past him. It attracted him, but it also made his palm itch.

She was feisty and even more so than he remembered from their time in Hawaii. It sounded, even to him, like he wasn't committed to her in Hawaii, and he supposed now, with more maturity and life experiences, things had changed. Probably because this was more than a temporary thing. Even though he was falling for Kai again, Seamus felt different now. This was for keeps.

Some days he loved her sassy ways, and others, not so much. When he looked at today's assignments, Kai was slated to lead a tour of the ranch for a family group of five. It was tacked onto her daily routine because she had requested it. Kai had been able to take Carter on a mock tour earlier this week, and since those were something Carter handled, Seamus didn't ask anything when Kai left the stables early, checking saddles before each party member mounted. And yet, his gut tingled, and not in a good way.

Seamus wasn't typically a micro-manager and tried to push off the wave of uneasiness that assailed his thoughts of her giving the tour today. He watched one of the hands, who also did tours, come out and help with one of the stir-rups. She had help, and even if Seamus had reservations because it was Kai's first official tour in relatively unfamiliar terrain, Carter had no such concerns. He was clear when answering Shay's question.

"She did well with me the other day, she has a co-rider today to make sure she retained all the important things, and he can fill in any answers she might not know yet. Chill, Shay. She's settling in great. We all love having her around."

Seamus hadn't found one thing Kai backed down from, and she had shown herself knowledgeable about horses and people. While it bothered him that his gut was a little unsettled, and he usually never ignored that feeling, he watched the prepping from the barn doors, and she was rock solid.

He chalked the unease to his desire that she be happy here. He needed to get to his own paperwork that was piling up and leave Kai to her job. She took a call, and after a few words, she finished, sliding the phone into her saddle bag. She was smiling and didn't look at all nervous. Seamus took his cue from her and turned back to the office, rubbing his burning gut. It was all right to ignore his misgivings this time. Maybe he was being overprotective.

Chapter Twelve

Kailani

Kai watched the buffalo warily. Ever since she had gotten the call from Avery saying the man who was to be her co-guide was stuck out in the far pasture with some duders, she was determined to show the family around alone. She'd settle in and enjoy them. Kai knew almost everything interesting and likely to be asked on the ranch. Carter's right-hand man was very good at training her. Besides, the family wouldn't likely ask something she didn't know. Ranching was ranching, whether in South Dakota or Hawaii.

She had thought to take Maverick with them as an extra set of eyes, but she didn't see him when they were ready to go, so she'd left without him. Maverick, Seamus' dog, was high energy and great company. He played with his humans and herded livestock and the people he claimed. Seamus said he was a black tri-color Australian shepherd from a litter that had never been registered. The dog was loyal and had taken a distinct liking to her.

Oh well, she knew what to do, where to go, and had nearly memorized the history of Red Eagle land and its people. She'd be fine. Seamus and Carter had agreed at the beginning of her employment that Seamus was not her boss. For obvious reasons. It had taken a considerable amount of pressure off her chest, untangling one aspect of their personal dynamic, but for times like today, that left no one to get direction from.

Carter had been specific that she needed one live session with a second. Renee and Avery had been equally adamant during a conversation about the lodge.

"Making sure that the guests are happy and entertained, if they want to be, is very important," Avery had said.

Feeling she had no other options, she called Carter, who was picking up supplies in town, left a message, and started the tour.

The sky was blue without one cloud to mar its expanse. Birds were sitting in trees, and the local vermin had scuttled into the thick groupings of underbrush to avoid the late afternoon heat. Kailani was glad she'd put her hair up in a ponytail because the back of her neck was already steamy. She would have been much hotter with her long, uncut hair lying as a curtain down her back.

The warm mountain air with a little bite of brisk wind was refreshing and made a person glad they were alive. She watched the family ahead of her, and they seemed to also enjoy that feeling of freedom and nature. The colts and fillies in her care had been kicking up their heels this morning, feeling the same exuberance they were all feeling now. In the short few weeks Kai had been at Red Eagle Ranch, she'd fallen in love with the place. Sharing that love with others was a great way to openly explore.

Now that they were nearly done exploring and ready to return home, the cattle were restless, which wasn't too abnormal. As Kailani talked about what seasons changing meant on the ranch with the cattle and ranch activities, the hair on the back of her neck stood up, a shiver ran through her body, and she was absolutely positive someone was watching her. She looked for a ranch hand, thinking possibly her co-guide Juan had made it after all, but she saw no one.

When the eldest daughter asked about the leaves changing and snowfall, Kai shook off the ominous feeling and admitted to the engaging family that she hadn't been at the ranch all her life.

"I've never even seen snow except on Moana Kea. I'm from a ranch in Hawaii. You know, the Big Island of Hawaii."

"Really?" said Sharon, the mother. "I thought you were a Red Eagle. You have the coloring, and they all act like you're one of them."

It was nice to know that others saw what she felt, but she had no intention of claiming to be Seamus' girl, no matter what he told his siblings.

"They're just an affectionate and inclusive family. It doesn't take long for you to feel at home here."

"We feel it too, just as guests," said Sharon. "So you get to see the beautiful fall colors for the first time, too? We live in Tennessee, and it is a glorious time of year. So beautiful."

"I'm excited to experience it for myself. Sorry to say it, but we need to get moving if we're going to take care of the horses and then give you time to get ready for dinner. Are you having it at the lodge or going into town?"

The group continued to chat and share about themselves as they began the ride back to the stables. As the family talked among themselves, interspersed with silent spells, Kai found her mind returning to Carter's rule about her first tour.

"You can go solo after you do one tour with a co-guide. We have a handful of people who do it in rotation, so grab one of them." She'd asked Juan, and he had agreed quickly enough, but now that he bailed, she'd have to deal with the fallout from Carter but not Seamus, thankfully. He wasn't her boss.

The tour was winding down, and things were smooth until the little group re-entered the part of the pasture that held the buffalo. As they left the fields and headed back to the riding stables, the cattle showed more restlessness, and even the horses were uneasy. The livestock, especially the buffalo, were fascinating to the family, and she tried to keep them from getting too close to the big brown and black beasts. As they weaved through the dispersing herd, she filled the little group in on why mating bison and beef worked so well.

"What's wrong with the horses, Kai?" asked the daughter, who seemed about ten.

"Lots of things can make animals skittish, but we're on our way back, so things should calm down any second."

Kai urged them on a little faster but not too fast, for some of the family weren't as proficient on horseback as others. Just as they could see the stables come into view, the horses took over and picked up their gait.

"Hold the reins, guys. These horses are trained, so they will walk back if held firmly. If you let the reins loose, they will take off home. I don't recommend that if you aren't an experienced rider."

Kai slowed down to make sure there wasn't a reason the herd was rumbling. The cattle seemed to have calmed down by the time she had reached the last copse of trees and was nearly cleared of it. She gathered her reins loosely, planning to take off behind the family, now halfway to their destination, when there was a rustling in the leaves overhead.

As she looked up, something fell from the sky and landed with a thud on the ground right in front of Susie, her mare. Her easy-going horse was immediately frightened, raising her front legs, and pounding the earth with her hooves while dancing around the fallen object.

Keeping her seat was nearly impossible, and Kai concentrated hard on keeping a firm hand on the reins while allowing Susie to give a wide space to whatever had scared them both. Susie demonstrated she wasn't as docile as others believed, causing Kai to squeeze her thighs to gain more control. She spoke softly, but the mare was too upset to hear her rider.

A shout came across the field in the opposite direction from the stables and house. Kai tried vainly to get her horse to calm down. Deciding the mare's unrelieved fear had to be surrounding whatever fell from the tree, Kai jammed her heels into the sorrel's flank, and after a shudder, the mare took off for home.

Kai reined Susie in just at the corral. Jumping off and turning her into the pen, Kai caught her breath and looked around at her guide party. Unfortunately, they weren't as oblivious to what had just happened as Kai had hoped. They could only stare at the mare and then at Kai.

"What was that in the tree? It sure looked like a snake from here," said the group's father.

"Might have been. We don't have snakes in Hawaii, so I didn't think about that. It might have just as well been a limb."

The couple of stable hands appeared to help the guests dismount and take the horses to be rubbed down, effectively ending the conversation. Kai said goodbye to the family, wished them well on the rest of their vacation and the trip home, then put them in transportation back to the lodge.

"I'll give Susie a minute to settle before I come back to rub her down."

She helped the stable hands to rub down the other horses, fed them a little, and turned them out into the corral until later, when all the horses were taken care of before they were put away for the night. Kai checked on her mares and foals, noting that a couple of the mama-baby pairs were ready to return to the larger fold. Once the foals were yearlings, they would return to another section to be hand gentled before breaking. She'd watch the new foals in the herd and see that they were acclimating and accepted by the pack. Horses were well known for their social skills, so she didn't anticipate any problems.

After all her chores were done, Kai realized how tired she was, likely due to the end of the afternoon tour. She sighed, relieved no one was hurt and headed for the house and a shower. She avoided places where Carter might have been, but she didn't have to because he had ridden out where this week's duders were camping to bring out more supplies.

Evidently, according to the stable hand Jayson, someone had dumped the bag of flour to put out the campfire this morning, saying it works on kitchen fires to smother them.

Kai rolled her eyes. Callen should have told them what to use to put out the fire. If it weren't that everyone would suffer, Carter wouldn't have gone out, but that's what you do when you have guests. She was all too aware of the need to be kind and protect your reputation. Kai had been doing that for years at home like she did today. She headed for the house feeling accomplished and proud of herself.

After the shower, Kailani set the table, looking up when Seamus and Carter came in. Avery spoke to the guys.

"Dinner in fifteen. If you hurry, Seamus, you'll have enough time to shower."

As expected, Renee was at ease with these big men because she had grown up with them, but so were Avery and Teagan. They had only known them a short while. Teagan had only a few weeks, and yet, they were comfortable. Kai wondered if her slight intimidation would completely go away whenever she was in the same room as these men. They each carried a commanding presence, only in a different way. Stryker was the most intimidating, and Kai was in awe of how Avery handled him in all his moods yet, wasn't intimidated at all.

Carter had already stopped at home to clean up, but Shay slowed as he passed Kailani to kiss her lips. Usually, he never slowed his step on his way to get the grime off.

"Be back in a few," he announced.

Kai touched her lips, and a slow, confident smile spread across her face. She'd be waiting for the second half, knowing she wouldn't be disappointed.

The conversation went where it usually did at the dinner table, recapping the day.

Seamus grumbled about paperwork. "Why do we have three pieces of paper for every transaction, order, or meeting note?"

Renee answered him without looking his way. "Because you guys tend to lose the first two copies," drawing a burst of laughter from Teagan.

"She's not wrong," said Avery. The men mumbled about being busy.

Declan talked about a student he thought was on the genius scale, which started a lively discussion.

"How can you be sure someone is on the genius scale when it is an arbitrary number," said Callen.

"Maybe, but that is how all measurement is. We make a standard and then use that as a measuring tool," defended Declan.

"But who's to say we shouldn't raise the bar? I mean, they say we don't use our brain to even close to its capacity," added Avery.

The opinions continued until Renee redirected the conversation to discuss changes she wanted to make at the Lodge. That began a whole other discussion about future plans for the ranch.

After a lull, Carter turned to Kai and asked, "How was your first guide trip with guests?"

Kai nodded. "Good. The family enjoyed the tour and asked really thoughtful questions. I had a fun time, and I'm sure they did too."

Avery said, "Oh, I'm so glad. I thought you'd cancel when Juan said he wouldn't make it back in time."

Carter asked conversationally, "So, who did you take with you?"

Kai didn't look at him. "No one."

"You went alone?"

She faced Carter. "I did. The family was already mounted and excited to go. I had proven I could do it alone yesterday. I checked my phone and told Jayson my itinerary. I left you a message, and then I went."

Carter reached back and pulled his phone from his pocket. "Yep, you did. But we need to discuss when a protocol is in place, you need to follow it."

"I tried to, Carter. If Juan had called before the group had shown up, I could have rescheduled or gotten a replacement. The problem was that when I found out, it was too late. Everyone was out of pocket. I had to make an informed decision."

Seamus asked, "And that conclusion told you to go without a second?"

"Yes. Look at it from my point of view. The family was already mounted and ready to go. They had spent a lot of money to vacation here and will likely do so again when they could have gone to any number of other places. The lodge's reputation would have taken a hit, and so would the ranch's. I know how important it is to keep your guests happy." She turned to Carter. "That's why you went out to bring more flour to the duders when one of them used the group's bag to douse a fire."

Stryker laughed, and the others snickered. "Damn, that's a new one. Did someone really do that?"

Renee answered with an exasperated sigh. "Someone did."

Carter shook his head. "Kai, you make it hard to chastise you when you have all the right answers. Well, I guess you did fine. It was only a precaution anyway." He leaned over and hugged Kai's shoulders. "But next time I say to do something a certain way, you do it."

"I'll try my best."

She grinned at Seamus when a grumbling sound came from deep in the man's chest. Her hand touched his, and he leaned over to share a kiss. He still wasn't happy, but it was Carter's area of authority. She had learned that the men kept to their respective responsibilities, coming together when areas overlapped or when planning and problem-solving. For a roomful of alpha males, it seemed to make things run smoothly. She needed that kind of solution with Seamus.

"These women are going to be the death of us," said Declan with a smile. "And I, for one, will die a happy man." He leaned over and kissed Teagan.

Teagan arched her eyebrow. "Good save, professor."

There was a knock on the kitchen door, and one of the cattle hands stepped into the kitchen, then the dining area. "Sorry to disturb you all, but I thought you'd like to know that Jayson went out after supper and looked to see what fell out of the tree. It was a huge rattler but a Timber, not a Prairie. You don't see Timber Rattlers around here."

"Fell out of the tree?" asked Seamus.

Kai nodded. "Yes, the cattle in the field, the group's horses, and then Susie was restless. Next thing I know, something," she waved her hand at the man they all called Chaps, "evidently, a snake, fell out of the tree above me."

"Where?" asked Carter.

"Just at the last outcropping before the stables. It upset Susie more than me, I think, so after trying to calm her, I gave the mare her head, and we rode in right behind the family."

"Anyway," said Chaps, "a Timber Rattler is a little north of his normal territory, so either we have them coming in now, or someone helped him here. This one's dead, though. Susie did a good job of stomping that sucker. I've checked her to make sure she wasn't bitten, and she seems okay so far. I called the game warden too, and they said to put it up, and they will come and have a look to-morrow."

Seamus spoke through lips drawn tight; his voice full of the realization that his girl had been in danger. "Kai don't forget we have snakes here. Something you aren't familiar with, I know, but be careful. If it rattles, it's poisonous."

"Thanks, Chaps," said Seamus. "I'll check in before going to bed tonight, just to be sure we're all good. I think we call this a fluke and go on. I'll do a little snake education with you this week, sweetheart. Then you won't worry about them when you come across one again."

The look Seamus gave Kai was easily interpreted to mean he wouldn't allow even those kinds of random incidents to happen. Kai could feel her independent streak push forward, but her love for this man forced her thoughts back into compliance.

If she showed him she was an intelligent woman, the kind he had wanted all along, he would begin to trust her judgment more about things. The additional side effect would be he wouldn't expect her to need so much watching and give her respect and space to do what she felt necessary in her life, knowing that would always include her sexy warrior Viking.

Seamus had gone suspiciously quiet the rest of dinner, and Kai was concerned that it wasn't the end of the discussion. This time, he would be coming from a place of a man who cared about her welfare, not as a job supervisor. She had good reasons for making the choice she did and had no problem standing by that, but when Seamus Red Eagle was in protection and education mode, she didn't usually come out unscathed.

She loved the man he was, but Kai did wonder if he was too intense. Did he expect too much from each of them to make this type of relationship work? And there was still the reason she came to South Dakota, near where she knew Seamus' people were. Seamus had not followed through with more questions about why she had come and then waited. She had appreciated the break in disclosure, but she expected that hiatus was over.

Kai looked at the profile of the man she had to admit she wanted now more than she had ever wanted him. Seamus was confident, and his work ethic was stellar. He took care of everyone. She needed that man more every day. Maybe she should stop tormenting them both and let him in the way he wanted into her life. He was still over-bossy, but maybe letting him in would lessen his concerns, and he would allow her more freedom to do what she knew she could. It was worth a thought or two.

Seamus gave her a deep, thoughtful sigh when she stood and leaned over to kiss him, preparing to go for a final look at her charges before shutting down for the night. His hand touched her waist and tightened when she would end the kiss quickly, extending the connection for a much longer, more satisfying joining.

Maybe that decision about telling him everything should be made sooner rather than later because she was about to combust from her need for his bossy, protective, satisfying self. But the intensity of her feelings frightened her sometimes. It was too much and not enough at the same time. She wondered if she should speak to Renee, Avery, and Teagan to see what advice they had.

Chapter Thirteen

Seamus

S Seamus watched his girl leave the room and knew she was it for him. The more time he spent with her, learning about her, the more convinced he was that he had to get a commitment from her. Shay wasn't ever going back to that carefree, every woman's sport, single status he'd once sworn he'd never leave. Once a certain opinionated, intelligent woman had entered his world, he was a goner. He knew it then, and he knew it now. When he had been introduced to Kailani Aka, all thoughts of grazing the green grassy fields filled with women eager to share his bed were over. She filled him up in a way he never knew a woman could. And she was in danger.

A random, out-of-its-habitat snake dropping from a tree wasn't too outrageous, but the timing was odd. Juan bailing out of helping her, the restless cattle, horses, then the snake all added up to the reason the hair on the back of his neck stood up. He'd caught first Stryker, then Carter's eye, then realized he wasn't the only one that experienced unease at the situation.

After Seamus made that fateful decision to finish his rehabilitation before contacting Kailani and all the events that followed, he was sure he'd never recover the bond and love they'd had, not with Kai and not to be reproduced with another woman. He'd been a defeated man with a lonely future ahead.

When he'd gotten the news about Kai's engagement, returning to play the field held no appeal for him. How could it? When he looked for a woman to fill his need for permanency, no one came close to the woman he'd had and lost. It was almost as though he was punishing himself for losing what was fast becoming most precious to him, yet, he'd allowed her to slip through his fingers.

Then, there she was, in his life again. After the initial show of his protective genes, Seamus tried to be very careful not to overwhelm her. Woo her while giving her what she had asked for, time. It was excruciatingly difficult to provide her with what she asked for when all he wanted to do was bundle her up, give her a cushy job and keep her safe from the world, but he did it because she asked him to.

And look what it got him. Kai had nearly been bitten by a poisonous snake she knew nothing about. Her horse could have hurt her in its own fear of the serpent, and he might have lost her. Was he overthinking this and overreaching the practical boundary of expectations with her? Yes. Damn, he needed to talk to Até and get a better perspective. He checked the clock. Nearly one a.m. there. He knew his father had been in bed for at least two hours.

He needed to search out brotherly advice before he made a misstep that he couldn't correct. After making a call to ensure his girl was still in the nursery stable and doing okay, Seamus went into the family room. Avery looked up when he walked in and quickly leaned over to kiss Stryker.

"I'm going to try that recipe that Libby told me about. Lots of cinnamon, butter, and brown sugar. Renee is in town, so why don't you come to help me make cinnamon toast bread, Teagan?"

"Why do you need..." Teagan looked up into Seamus' face and nodded. "I'm not much of a baker, but I'd love to watch you."

Declan snagged a kiss and patted her butt as she crossed in front of him. Both men watched their women leave the room and then refocused their attention on Seamus.

"Shay, pull up a seat. Is Kai still out in the barn?"

He nodded. "She is. Guess one of the mares will likely deliver in the next few days, so she's giving her some extra attention."

Carter walked in with Callen carrying a six-pack, and all the men sat popping tops. "She is the perfect person for the nanny stables," said Carter. "My concern is when we stop foaling season. I don't think we have but two left. Then we'll keep them for a week or so, but I'd say, before the end of this month, we'll be done. We don't start breaking yearlings until the spring. Got a plan for where we put her then?"

Stryker spoke into the quiet. "I've been thinking about that. Don't we have calving in November? We can figure out something for October, but encourage her to help with the calving. If she could watch and know when a cow is ready, we could keep them close. We won't be searching for so many as in the past. That alone will be a great help."

Seamus stared at the can in his hand as though it had the answer to all his trouble. "I think if she works on the ranch with specific jobs, she will be happy. But the question is, can I make her want to stay?"

"What?" asked Callen. "Has she said anything about going?"

"No, but I'm afraid that the man I am, what I expect from my woman, might scare her off. Run her off." Seamus took a drink.

Declan leaned back, always the thoughtful one. "Seamus, you have always been the gentle giant. Why would you worry that she's changed her mind about you?"

"Because I've been holding back who I am since she showed up. I went all alpha on her that first night, but because she shied away, I pulled back. I don't want to rock the boat, but..." He shook his head. "She's only had a single dose of me for a month. I'm talking much longer than that now. And there will be many times I will take over in our life."

Stryker put his can on the end table. "Have you asked her?"

Seamus just leaned back in his seat, right ankle propped on left knee, and stared.

"I take that as a no," continued Stryker. "Look, I tried to hold back my attraction to Avery because she worked for me, and at first, that was a good idea. But when it became a mistake, I declared my beginning feelings and backed away. Once you commit, you have to be all in. She expects that, and a woman deserves to know you aren't going to change your mind about anything important."

"I don't have to have it all at first, but I think she's the one. No, I know she is. If my overbearing attitude knocks her off her feet badly, I've burnt that bridge."

Callen smiled. "You're a goner, man. I didn't know much about Kai when you were in Hawaii, because I was off at college, but the look on your face tells me you have it as bad as the other two. I'd claim her and go from there. She'll come around."

Carter laughed. "That's why you're still playing the field, man. A woman needs to know she's special to you. That even though you are overprotective at times, it's because you can't imagine life without her. And after you have officially claimed her and later need to spank her ass for getting into some mess she had no business getting involved in, she'll allow it because you are the only one in the world with that privilege. She'll know to her very marrow that should anyone be so stupid as to consider laying a finger on her, you will send him into orbit without the compliment of a rocket."

The room of men all stared at Carter. "You got yourself a sweetheart we don't know about, Carter?" asked Declan.

"No. If I ever claim a woman, you would all know it. No one keeps a secret long around here."

Seamus watched Carter for a long moment before nodding and sitting back. "Yeah, I imagine that's right." He sat his empty can down. "So do I continue to be who I am, full on this time, and risk her response, or do I hang tight a while longer? I can be patient."

An even, sweetly familiar voice spoke from the doorway. "I'd say, do what feels right. If it didn't turn her off the first time, it wouldn't likely do it now. But if you're afraid to take a chance, well... then that's on you, I guess. I need a man who isn't afraid to show more than his gentle, accepting side."

The men swung their heads toward the doorway and saw Renee, Teagan, Avery, and Kai standing at the entrance. The women walked around Kai, leaving her standing alone, as if they had choreographed it. Kai walked over to Seamus and grinned mischievously, staring down at his lap.

"Is this seat taken, sir?"

"Yes, ma'am, it is now." Seamus pulled her into his lap and shared a kiss that showed he was more than ready to take his place in a relationship he was all in on.

His memory must be faulty. Otherwise, the woman he remembered with so much passion had been replaced by this Kai, who was an inferno. She was the most incredible woman he'd ever known, and now, they had just given each other a tonsillectomy that he was having trouble recovering from. His whole body was on fire, and he couldn't have been happier.

The others resumed talking around them as Seamus looked enquiringly into her eyes. He could see some of her seriousness shine through.

"You sure, sunshine? I don't want to force you into something you don't want, but I need to be who I am. Who we can be together. I'm willing to compromise but not on everything."

"I'm more than ready to start to see if this works for us."

He dropped a hard, fast kiss on her lips. "Good. Take a shower, and I'll be up there in fifteen minutes. Be ready to talk."

"Talk? But I'd hoped we could do a little more than that."

"I guess that all depends on how the talking turns out. Now go on. I'm starting the count as soon as you hit the top of the stairs."

Kai stood with a hint of a pout and turned towards the door when Carter stopped her. "Hey, Kai, how was our mama tonight?"

"Good, but she seems a little uneasy. Her teats have been waxing today, so I wouldn't be surprised if she dropped her foal tomorrow."

"I'll have the guys check on her every couple of hours through the night. Thanks."

"Sure. She's a sweet thing. I'm going to get the scent of horse off me."

Kai stopped to talk to Avery. Seamus swatted her butt.

"Get going, woman. I'm coming in after you."

Kai put her hands on her hips and stared at Seamus. He gave her a look of his own. Seamus hid his smile when she dropped her hands in frustration.

"Night, everyone."

KAILANI

Kai couldn't help the thrill that ran through her when Seamus responded to her words tonight. She knew he was hesitant, but she hadn't known what to do with that knowledge since the Seamus she had known in Hawaii was different from this one. This Seamus was more cautious and careful, and Kailani had allowed that because she didn't know if she was ready to handle the fully in charge Red Eagle.

As she stepped from the shower, her eyes partly closed, she reached for the towel she had left handy and didn't feel it. As Kai groped in front of her expecting to land on cloth, her hands landed on a hard man. Then a towel wiped her face before strong, efficient hands rubbed her down from top to bottom.

"Hey, I can dry there."

"I'll be done before you can finish complaining. Now hush and spread 'em."

She did as directed, her face flaming by the time he was done. Seamus dropped the towel and reached in between her thighs. He slid past her new landing strip that she tried to keep shaved, and his fingers spread her wide.

"Seamus, you don't have to, um... mmm, yes, right there."

"Yeah, feel good?"

"So good. But you don't have to do this."

"True," he focused on her clit. "Put your hands on the counter and push out, baby. Yes, just like that. Now quiet. The bathroom echoes."

Kai could feel her breath hitching as he worked on her. Her whole core was heated, and her need to come was growing. "Please let me come. Don't stop."

"Oh, I'm not edging tonight, baby. You can have all the orgasms you want. But for this one, no more talking, or daddy is removing his fingers." He demonstrated by stopping and sliding them out of her pussy.

"No," she whispered her raspy words. "Don't stop."

He kissed her back, and she could feel the goosebumps that rose over her skin. He slapped her backside twice.

"You're lucky I don't oversee the ranch tours, or your ass would be red hot right now. Disobeying me when the rules are designed for your safety will not happen again, will it, my little sweetheart?" He ran his fingers through her channel again, tweaking her clit.

Her heavy breathing had calmed, but now he was ratcheting her libido. "No, I'll try to pay more attention if I can."

"Yes, you will, or daddy is going to spank your perky backside cherry red." He scooped her up and carried her to the bedroom, then he reverently put her in the center of the bed. "Hands and knees, baby."

Kai quickly complied. Another two swats landed on her upturned bottom, and his hand slid back into place. This time he leaned over to tweak her nipples that were protruding dark and firm.

"I love these nips. They are luscious and firm and all for me to play with. Spread your legs wider, baby. I need to view my playing field."

She spread her thighs more and begged him to finish. "Please, please, I can't hold on much longer."

He pulled his fingers from inside her and flicked her clit intently. "Then come, sunshine."

His slick finger went into her dark back entrance and was soon followed by two fingers wiggling inside her bottom. He knew she loved back-door play, and she came as he fully introduced the second digit. He nursed her climax with kisses and fingering. Kai wasn't sure she'd ever sustained for as long as this time.

Breathing hard, she rolled over and smiled at him. "Did you get your shower?"

"Yep, but I have a feeling we're going to need another before we get going in the morning." He reached over to the side table drawer and reached in. Shay made a face and then leaned closer. His shoulders dropped. "Might be out of condoms."

"In the bathroom drawer. I didn't want to come up wanting."

He ignored the heavy pun because he was on a mission, but the impish grin told him she was proud of her response. "You didn't, hmm? You're fucking perfect for me."

Kai giggled. "Because I stocked up on condoms? That was all about me, big guy."

"Then let me continue the trend. I'll be right back."

The sink turned on and within a minute, the drawer opened and there was a long, low whistle before he strolled out with a long strip of condoms.

"You bought fancy and enough for a high school football team after winning the state championship."

Her laugh was music to his ears. He was never letting her go. He dared Rufus fucking Paolo to try to interfere.

He rolled a condom on. "One of these days, I'm going to dispense with these things."

"I'm on the pill. I guess we could now if you want."

"I'm more comfortable with you knowing I'm clean before I do that. But the day is coming."

He leaned over and kissed her deeply, taking it from a lip-to-lip event to a full mouth expedition. His hungry eyes smiled at her with a kind of foreknowledge of coming events.

"Ready for more?"

Kai wiggled. "Yes, so much more."

"Mmm, so what did you have in mind?"

"Right now? More loving."

Seamus introduced his tongue between her thighs, lapping her goodness, extracting another orgasm before he slipped into her wetness. Kai couldn't think straight. All she could do was feel, and this felt like coming home; passionate, comforting, right.

The slapping of flesh on flesh, kissing her lips and her nipples in turn, sucking as he slowly pumped, grabbing her hips as he took her hard. The high-pitched careening of her next orgasm was followed by a deep, rumbling male moan. Collapsing on her before rolling over to land beside her in the bed, Seamus brought down his breathing and kissed his still heaving breathless Kai. Rolling off the side of the bed, he disposed of the condom, ran the water, and walked out with a washcloth.

Seamus was a gentleman. Kai knew he would do that, as he had done it every time they'd had sex in her bungalow. Their connection was smoking hot. That worked for her. If this was her reward for letting him pull out his possessive, protective, bossy self, it was more than worth it. The warmth of the cloth soothed her tender flesh as he carefully cleansed her.

"When I'm putting a baby in you, this will only happen after you've held my sperm for a while. When we're ready, I don't want to take any chances with impeding progress."

"You know that isn't how it works, right?"

"I know we are hedging our bet."

"Shay, we are a long way from making babies."

"Maybe, or maybe you are in denial. We'll see who is right."

"Whatever." Seamus grabbed hold of her thigh and rolled her toward him. He landed two smarting swats to her butt. "Hey!"

"Don't 'whatever,' daddy."

"Oh," she giggled, "We're playing again, huh? What do you plan to do?"

He dropped a kiss and barreled over her to land on the far side of the bed.

"Me? Oh, I thought you'd lay with me and explain what brought you here in the first place. I'm damn glad you came to the ranch because otherwise, I would have gone there to find you. If it weren't for your grandmother, I would have still thought you were married."

"Married? Now that would be interesting, given I'm here with you. Okay. You told me why you didn't call after the accident and then later. So, it's only fair to give you the whole story."

Seamus laid on his back and drew Kai close, placing her cheek on his chest and his chin on her head.

"I came because you told me to."

"Go on," he encouraged as he smoothed her hair away from her face.

"You said I should come here if I was in trouble or needed anything. I didn't know what else to do, so I came. Then when I got here, I was afraid to just barge in with no means of support or a place to stay. My plan was to work, get an apartment, then knock on your door, so to speak. I didn't think you were here, but I was banking on you being right and your family being available to help me."

"Okay, that was a good call. Now, what happened that you needed help, baby? What was your Nan talking about?"

"A man, his whole family, wants my grandfather to sell our ranch. We have acres of land, and over the years, commercial projects have tried to have us sell. Usually, after we turn them down, they eventually stop trying. Then, three years ago, this man, Clifton Paolo, from the Paolo Tradewinds Resort, tried many ways to get our land, but without a result."

Kailani went silent as she relived Clifton Paolo's demands, trying to get her grandfather to sell to him. He wasn't even Hawaiian, and demanding her family sell was unheard of, yet, this man had done just that.

"I'm sorry, baby. Then what happened?"

"Then, a couple of years ago, he sent his daughter, Marla, who tried to entice my brother, Mana. They dated for a while, but unfortunately for her and her family, Mana met his future wife on one of their dates, teaching hula to children. He went back later and talked with her, taking her on a date, and within a week, he dumped Marla. Her family was furious. They tried to say my brother had broken his promise to marry her, but at a party, my brother had made it clear in front of witnesses that he enjoyed Marla, but she wasn't the one for him. So, that was that."

"Bastards. Someone always wants to take what others have instead of making what they have work for them."

"True, but some people don't understand the word no. Anyway, we thought that was all. We were mistaken."

"Seems to me that you would have made it clear that either they left your family alone or something might happen."

Kai shoved his pec. "You can't tell people that. It sounds like a threat."

"Or a promise," he said ominously.

"Yes, well, I only have two brothers and don't want them to go to jail. Dad is not as strong as he used to be. Anyway, about six months ago, Rufus came around. I hadn't met him because he'd been away at college and something else, so it wasn't until he started taking me places or escorting me, more to the truth of it, did I learn who he was."

"Kai. If he hurt you..."

She placed her hand on his as she shook her head. "Seamus, he didn't."

Kai snuggled in closer. "At first, Rufus was kind and offered to take me to things that I like, community events, art displays, plays, and that kind of thing. Then he started telling people we were together. I didn't think that much about it, and if I were asked, I always set people straight about the relationship or lack thereof. Then things began to change at the beginning of last month. I overheard him tell someone on his cell phone that he would kidnap me and use me for ransom. The ranch for my life."

Seamus' head shot up from resting on the top of her head. "The hell you say. What did your family do?"

"They told me to leave, but I thought it was all talk. Rufus is all talk but not much follow-through. Except right before I came here. After I overheard his conversation, I refused to go anywhere with him. Late afternoon on the day before I left, Rufus tried to grab me off the street. I was in the middle of a rush of tourists when he said something to me with his face shoved up against my ear. I swear it sounded like he said, 'I could be your fantasy or your worst nightmare.'"

Seamus' muscles were stiff and taut. "Damn, sweetheart. I'll fly there myself and take care of him."

"No, I don't want him to know where I am. He could turn on my family, my grandparents."

"I hope you reported it."

"I did, but tourists don't know what to do, so plenty of them watched everything as it happened and aren't trackable. One man, who I'm sure was military, knocked Rufus to the ground. Rufus took off in his car, but I think the police picked him up. I took out a protection order. The guy, Mr. Creighton, who helped me, took me to the police station to file a report, but, again, all my witnesses were tourists."

"So all gone or unidentifiable."

"Right. The guy who helped me did leave his name with the police. He also said he was leaving soon. He apologized for not seeing Rufus do more than harass me." She shrugged. "So no eyewitnesses. That's part of the reason why I thought he was military. Anyway, I didn't know what to do, so I packed my bags and headed here."

Seamus kissed the top of her head. "His first name is Creighton. I've met him. Nice guy. And I'll have to send him something when I find him in appreciation for taking care of my girl. I still want to annihilate this Rufus person. I'm also upset you didn't even try to call me or the ranch as soon as you were having trouble, but I get it. I really do. I was an ass about my injury, and even though I feared you would feel obligated to stick with me if I couldn't recover fully, I also know that you would have never been put in the Rufus position if I had called you. I have that to work through on my own." He kissed her again. "But now, we have a different issue to deal with."

"What, exactly?"

His laugh permeated the area. "Worried?"

"Maybe. Should I be?"

"I wouldn't think so. I was just going to do this." Pulling her up closer, his kisses started at her lips, her tongue sweeping into his warm eager mouth, engaging his tongue in a dueling match. "Or this..." He kissed down her jawline, finding the ticklish spot below her ear on her jawline, and kissed it, causing giggles to erupt. He fucking loved hearing them.

"Or, maybe we might go here."

He slid lower, his hands cupping her breasts, offering the nipples to his awaiting mouth one after the other, sucking, licking, squeezing, loving. His feelings for Kailani were so strong that he was half-hard even when he disagreed loudly with her. He fucking loved everything about her, except Kai's penchant for doing her own thing when it put her in danger.

That was a habit he was intent on curbing in her while trying to make her so happy she wouldn't leave him, even when things settled down at her family home. He wanted her here, with him. That started with satisfying her completely and making her so hungry for his touch that she couldn't imagine not having him with her. It started now.

He slid further down, mouth salivating, eyes on her hidden prize.

Chapter Fourteen

Kailani

Kailani could feel herself floating back to earth. She'd been with Seamus before, been the grateful recipient of Seamus' attention for long moments. He'd edged her for what seemed like hours, then brought her to a fast and furious climax. He'd gently claimed her as though he were the most privileged of men, and she was made of the finest china.

After they had napped, Kai had taken him in her mouth. Loving him felt so erotic that she thought she'd orgasm while giving him pleasure. That had never happened before because she'd only offered this man that kind of loving. Shay was pulling out his third condom to "fuck her hard and fast," to quote him. She believed him.

The man had more stamina than she could ever hope to have, and patience? He could play the long game, probably forever, if he wanted to. Kai was flagging, and as much as she loved a good romp, she was losing momentum. He slapped her backside.

"Hands and knees, baby." Three more spanks bounced off her fit backside, then he kneaded her ass, and she could feel her arousal make her thighs wet and the exposed areas were cooled by the air.

Kai complied with an admonition. "I'm running out of steam here, so if you want to finish well, do it now. Otherwise, if I slow down..."

Kai tried to balance losing control in his exuberant lovemaking and staying present enough to enjoy the ride. She sucked in air through her teeth when his broad fingers swiped some of her wetness. She squealed when those same fingers rimmed her dark back entrance and pressed one fingertip more insistently. She whined at the sensations the effort was delivering.

"Making love isn't supposed to be this strenuous, Seamus."

"You think not? If you're tired, then I'm fucking you right."

He pounded his pelvis against her backside, and as she stretched to accommodate his pistoning cock, she began to feel the tingle that heralded yet another release of fluid. She'd lost count of how many times he had fired her up. She couldn't believe she was gearing up for another trip to paradise. She was too tired. And yet...

"Come for me, Kai. Clench my cock."

"No," she heard herself whine, "I can't."

"You can. When daddy says come, he means it. Rub your clit, baby, and don't stop."

"Too much."

"Then do it gently, but you will do it. You know what naughty will get you."

She touched her clit, the little bit of flesh that held her most reactive nerve center. Kai was sure she would be too sensitive and was surprised to feel the most sensitive bit still out of its hood, touchy, yes, but not painfully so.

"Do it, Kailani. Do it now."

Seamus lightly spanked her ass again. Then he pinched her buttocks. Kai squealed. She was drenched in her juices and craved him so much that she did as he directed. She was getting close, and her little moans and grunts were getting louder. She'd be ashamed if she didn't know they weren't the only couple enjoying each other's company.

"Get there, baby. I'm approaching the landing pad."

He slapped her right buttock once, then twice. When he landed a third heavy-handed smack to her ass, his fingertips tapped her hot, raw pussy. She flew, not as traumatic as the first ones, but still enough to clench his cock extra tight and for her to hear his sharp intake of breath, her buttocks contracting.

"Damn, you're strangling me," his last words before his climax took him hard.

His harsh, raspy release thrilled Kai. She loved when she could help in his escape to nirvana. Seamus was always working on her satisfaction in the bedroom. She wanted to make sure he was finding pleasure as well. His muscular toned body left only a few soft places on his body. However, the safety and power he exuded and the heat he radiated created a cocoon of protection. Something that she needed so much in her life. Her reaction was almost orgasmic.

She heard him say something but wasn't sure what it was as she cuddled down on the fresh-smelling sheets and pillowy comforter. Her tongue licked his nipple.

"Behave and sleep, little girl," was his gruff response.

She smiled as she closed her eyes.

One more sexy time in the wee hours of the morning had Kai trying to force her brain to focus when her alarm went off. Climbing back through the dense disorientation was a battle. She must have dozed again because the next thing she knew, she smelled coffee.

"Gimme," she grumbled.

"Sit up and prove you can hold the cup."

She shook her head. "You hold it."

Seamus laughed as he held the cup to her lips once she sat up. "Is daddy's baby tired this morning? Take a sip. Careful, it's hot."

"Mmm, so good." She reached for the cup to hold it. "What time is it, and what day is it?"

"It's six-thirty on Saturday morning."

"Let me sleep in."

"I would, sunshine, but I think we're going to get a new family member soon. Mama Cassie is restless and beginning to show signs of labor. I want you to be there when this one comes. It's an experience you don't want to miss, and these mares are comfortable with you. I think it would go a long way toward keeping her calm. So get moving, girl. I have breakfast downstairs waiting for you."

He kissed her, and Kai closed her mouth and shook her head no. Pulling her head back, a dainty hand landed over her mouth.

She said, "Morning breath."

His determination shone on his face as he moved her hand. "Nope," he kissed her again. "Tastes like coffee and my baby. Nice combo. I need another taste." He took her cup from her hands and placed it on the dresser before kissing her long and hard. "Now get a move on, woman."

Kai watched this gorgeous specimen of a man, her man, with his magnificent ass, take confident strides from the room. She heard him walk down the hallway and take the stairs to the kitchen below. No hesitation, no concerns. Seamus carried his confidence as a man fully in charge of his world. He was sure

she would follow him now and wherever he led. She needed him like she needed air to breathe. Kai determined to do whatever it took to keep Seamus wanting what she could give him.

Now how to make that package sweeter.

As Kailani entered the nursery side of the stable, she sensed an air of anticipation and seriousness. Carter raised his head when she entered far enough for
him to acknowledge her. Several other mares were turned into the paddock to
lessen the activity in the stable.

"She's doing well, but I don't think Mama Cassie is too happy with anything right now. She went into labor nearly an hour ago, and I'm not sure of the
foal's position right now. We'll just have to wait and watch. You good staying
with her for a bit? I have a few other chores to get done."

"Sure, but what if she gets upset or does something, I don't know, un-horse-
like?"

"Then you call me. This is her first foal, so I don't know how she'll do. We'll
just have to wait and see. You good with that?"

She shrugged. "Of course."

"Okay, you don't pass out when you see blood or anything, right?"

"Um, no, except I've never seen a horse give birth before, so I can't be positive."

"Oh, you'll do fine. Okay, call me with any changes, and I'll see you later.
Call me if there is any blood, a rush of water, or if you see her lay down."

Kailani felt like she had been sitting and talking nonsense while petting the
mama for a while. When she heard the stall door open, she looked to see Seamus squat beside her. His voice was low and soothing. He reached out and ran
his hand over Mama Cassie's belly.

"How're you doing, baby?"

"Good, but I need to get up and walk around, go to the bathroom. Do you
think you could stay here for a moment?"

"Honey, you should have asked someone to relieve you. You've been here
for a few hours, and I imagine she's getting ready to finish this."

"It's okay. But I really need to go." She tried to show her sense of urgency by
using his thigh to push off. Her legs were numb. "Carter checked a little bit ago
when she laid down, and he said he'd be back. It was about time, but she was
doing well."

"Go on. Take your time. I'm going to hang out with you now."

Kai leaned down and dropped a loving kiss on his lips. "I'll be back shortly."

She took her full bladder and stiff legs to the room next to the office that held a full, albeit small, bathroom with a shower, toilet, and sink.

"All the comforts of home," she said to no one. This was beginning to feel like home, well, except it was nothing like Hawaii.

Feeling better, Kai went to the office, where cold water and pop were kept inside the small refrigerator. She grabbed one water and one cola, then reached up in the cabinet beside the little sink and coffee pot. She snagged two granola bars and headed back to the stalls.

Mama Cassie was snorting and sounded restless. "She okay?" asked Kai as she handed the pop to Seamus and a bar.

"Yeah, she's voicing her opinion about you leaving and me being a poor substitute."

"What?"

"Honest. The minute you left, she got dissatisfied. It's your gentle touch, baby." He leaned down to kiss her lips. "Animals aren't dumb. They know a good thing when they see it."

"But all I did was talk about nothing and rub her."

"Seems that's what she wants. Drink your water and eat the snack, then I want to get her moving a little. I'd hoped she would progress better than she has."

"Is something wrong? Seamus, nothing can happen to her. Can't you call a vet or something?"

Seamus drew Kai near and kissed the top of her head. "She's fine, baby. More like you relaxed her so much her labor stalled, so let's get her blood pumping more. See if we can't get her more interested in dropping this little guy."

Together they finished their refreshments and walked the mare some. Slow and sure until it was apparent she was ready to get down to business. Seamus looked at Kai with loving eyes.

"Okay, let's give her some of your calming voice and gentle hand rubs to keep her from getting too agitated because we are about to welcome a new addition."

Seamus felt around the great girth of the animal and seemed to listen to her belly for an extended time. "What a good girl. I think she's getting some good, strong contractions, and she is a healthy mare, so this should be smooth, but you never know."

The next moment there was a gush of fluid, and immediately following that came a little nose and front hooves. The rest of the foal appeared quickly. Seamus pulled at the sack, tearing it from around the colt, pulling it over the animal's head, and clearing its muzzle of anything impeding the little one's first breaths.

"And there you go. A beautiful new member of the ranch."

Mare and foal were peacefully recovering. Seamus glanced over at his too-quiet girl and found tears coursing down her cheeks.

"Aww, baby. They're fine." He reached for her.

She sniffed as she nodded. "I know. It was so incredible."

Kai allowed Seamus to pull her to him and settle into his comfortable big arms and warm as a heater chest, her eyes locked onto the peaceful scene of mother and baby sharing scents and bonding. Soon, the rest of the clan began to show up, eager to be introduced to the adorable foal and to comfort and encourage the mare on her firstborn.

"Well, Kai," said Carter, "One more this season, and you can take a little time off before we start with the calving. If you don't mind helping, we are trying to not have to go hunting as often for the calves this year."

"Really?" she asked with enthusiasm. "I'd love to help. This is more paniolo work than I've ever gotten to do." She turned a beaming face to Seamus leaning against the tack wall, arms folded with a smile on his face.

Seamus didn't say anything, but Declan and Callen started talking about what else she could do. She glanced back at Seamus as he spoke in response to their offerings.

"Kai will not be helping with the duders, Callen. When you get your girl, you'll understand. And Declan, you don't even let Teagan work with those college guys."

"You got that right. Those interns look like they haven't ever seen a woman before or have but haven't touched one."

Stryker chuckled as he sauntered into the stable. "Sounds a little frightening. Next time you let them back, give us a heads up so we can plan a vacation or something."

"Yeah, yeah. No, I just meant that if Kai needed something to fill her time, I have prep work she can help with."

"No," said Renee, "Avery and I have some reorganizing that she can help with. It makes more sense because she helped run the lodge at her family's ranch."

Seamus pushed off the wall with the foot he had propped against it and leaned forward to snag Kai about the waist when she tried to move out of his way.

"No, she's taking a break, helping where she wants but mostly taking a break. Then, we will get ready for calving."

He dropped a kiss on her lips to stop any conversation she may have been about to start.

"I mean it, Kai."

As his stern words grumbled in her ear, they shot a hard shiver of anticipation through her. If she disobeyed him, he would have something to say about it. Shay was a man's man, which made him this woman's dream. Hell, if other women were honest, he would be theirs too. But she had to tease him.

"Actually, I might like putting some hormonal, immature guys in their place. No matter what their ages are."

He pinched her ass. "We'll work on that idea later."

She hissed and stomped her foot, drawing the eyes of almost everyone in the room. "Stop. Everyone is watching," she hissed.

He looked up and back down at Kai. "I could swat your ass."

"No!"

"I didn't think so." He rubbed out the sting. "Let's leave Carter with his charges, and we'll go work on ideas for your next few weeks."

"But there is one more mare."

"I know. You can work with her and get the foaling over, then I want you to take a break. Not playing here."

"Well, I have to call my family and find out if everything is okay for me to return."

The others were leaving as well, and soon, it was just Carter, Kai, and Seamus. He finished talking with Carter as Kailani made a quick detour to have a final look in the stall. It was such a beautiful sight. Seamus slid his hand to the small of her back, drawing her into his hold as he led her out of the building.

"So what are you going to do with your free time?"

"You were serious?" her shocked tone seemed to say everything.

Seamus shook his head. "Completely serious. Calving won't start for a month, and we've already moved the last of the cattle for now, so this is everyone's downtime.

"So you aren't working, either?"

"Well, I run the ground operations on the ranch, so I don't have time off, but it is slower. No duders until Thanksgiving week."

"Then I want something to do."

Seamus sighed. "Woman, why is it that you can't take a break? You act like I'm making a statement about your abilities. I'm not. I'm expressing my desire to give you some free time. You're my girl; if I did what I wanted, you'd be in the house or riding with one of the other ladies and having a good time. I get you want to work, but I don't have to like it. Especially when you don't give yourself enough credit and don't expect we do either. Your work ethic and ability to settle those mares, babies and yearlings are impressive. But this is how it is on a working ranch. Chores ebb and flow according to the time of year. There's always something to do but sometimes you have to go looking for it."

"That's sounding more and more like caveman mentality," Kai accused him.

He held his hands up and opened the gate to the workhorses. "I understand that, so I'm trying hard not to be that person on the outside." Closing the gate firmly, he reached out and ran his fingers down her jawline. "I worry that something will happen to you when I'm not there to fight your demons or catch you if you fall." He raised his hand to stop her words. "Figuratively and practically."

"Yeah, well... that's so sweet. Thanks. But really, I can't sit around doing nothing all day."

"I get it. Okay, how about you check with Carter but take a few days off first, or he won't be happy about finding you something to do. Hang out with the girls at the lodge or something."

"Fine."

"Thanks, Sunshine." The kiss was sweet and light when it started but left both breathless when they finally separated. "Mm, I need to get you back in bed."

"You have things to do, cowboy, but I think a little bedcover rodeo is possible tonight."

"Damn, now I won't be able to do much work without thinking about what events we can have later."

Kailani laughed, her throaty, sexy sound nearly bringing Shay to his knees. He dropped a hard, fast kiss on her cheek.

"I have to walk away now, baby, or we won't be doing anything but hitting the sheets."

She turned and stepped in front of him, giving Seamus a clear shot at her swaying ass. The sound of his hand clapping on her jeans-covered backside drew a wide-eyed backward look from Kai.

"Meanie."

"I'm not the tease around here."

She laughed her seductive laugh and waltzed away. Yeah, he was a goner.

RUFUS SMILED. FINALLY, he'd caught a break. That cousin on his father's side had finally done something right. Warning him off of Kailani was the information he had been looking for. South Dakota, huh? Red Eagle, what a lame last name. He was likely as dumb as his name if he had let Frank Cassini know anything about him.

It didn't matter because if that is what it took, a memory that Frank had recalled that Red Eagle was a ranch owner in South Dakota, then it was enough. Frank didn't do things on purpose; he simply didn't see the significance in the things he knew. In this case, he never suspected that telling where Red Eagle was would put the last piece in the puzzle Rufus had been trying desperately to finish.

Now he knew where Kailani Aka was. Her family had said that she was visiting a military friend she'd met some years ago. Male or female wasn't answered, and he couldn't find that link that would identify where she went. But now, as soon as he saw where the ranch was, he would be on a plane to retrieve his runaway bride. Then, the Aka ranch was as good as his, not his father's. It was time to be his own man, and he would start with the Aka property.

How dare Cassini imply that he was harassing Kailani. She was for him. He'd force the ungrateful woman to sign a prenuptial, then marry him. On their honeymoon, she'd have an accident, and it would all be over. The ranch would be his as soon as the other owners were taken care of or convinced to sell for next to nothing. The Aka family had missed their chance to do this the easy way. Now it was going to cost them dearly.

If the family still resisted, after a bit of time, they would begin to die off; old age, accident, lousy health, whatever worked. His father wanted that ranch, but Rufus would own it. If he paid well, then Rufus would sell it to him. No one stopped a Paolo from getting what he wanted. Not even another Paolo.

He got excited when he thought of the fear Kailani would feel when she realized he owned her. Her family wouldn't be so noble after he finished with them. He might even mess with the Red Eagles for keeping his future wife and gold mine from him. Teach them a lesson in sticking their nose into another man's business.

He opened up his computer. Now, to find where Kailani Aka was hiding.

Chapter Fifteen

K*ailani*
The things Seamus had later come up with to occupy her time were lame. Read a book. She did that at night or in the evenings if there was nothing else she wanted to do. Call her friends? Really? Kai loved her family and had a few close friends, but they all said she'd be an idiot if she didn't put her whole heart into loving her Viking warrior. Besides, the time difference made that a delicate thing to do.

It had been a few days, and Kai began to have the funniest feeling that someone was watching her. She didn't tell anyone because it was a crazy thought. They were ten miles from the nearest hub of civilization, and no one would go down a side road to watch people on a cattle ranch. There were guests in the lodge, which was probably the reason she felt people were watching her because they likely were. Kai ignored the fact that the inn was almost half a mile away.

She just had too much time on her hands, she kept telling herself, so to change that, she headed off on a horse to the hot springs on the ranch. It was a distance, but she could check the fence line on the way just so she wasn't squandering her time. She checked her supplies, including a skimpy swimsuit she put on under her practical jeans and a long-sleeved shirt, grabbing a towel and lunch before heading out.

The hair on the back of her neck rose. Why was she so jittery today? Maybe because she didn't tell Seamus or Carter where she was going? She did tell Chaps as he brought out Susie. Why? She wasn't entirely sure, but she didn't like telling everyone where she went all the time. Chaps would know if she were gone too long and give her cell a ring.

Kai had found out on the afternoon of the snake that Susie didn't mind taking charge and dealing with a problem if it presented itself. Kai needed a spunky ride. Susie was that. Chaps nodded as he gave Kai a hand up and told her not to worry about snakes in the trees. He had talked to the neighboring ranches and found out one of the rancher's sons had a rattler go missing. So nothing to worry about. That was a relief. Snakes were not something she was familiar with or wanted to be.

It was getting chillier these days and near freezing at night. It was crucial that she not stay out too late, arousing Carter or Seamus' concern. Kai wasn't used to wasting time when everyone else around her worked. It didn't help much that they worked more leisurely because they still had a plan for the day. Kai knew certain things had to be done before winter came on the ranch, but everyone seemed to know their part in the preparation. Everyone but her.

At breakfast today, even the lodge, which was nearly empty, was in preparation mode. The manager had housekeeping doing a thorough clean and their landscaper/gardener preparing things for winter. Even Teagan was taking her off time to prep the business books for the end-of-year and fourth-quarter reporting, so checking the fence line seemed like an excellent way for Kai to help.

As she rode to the hot springs, she saw a flock of birds fly away as though they were spooked. Kai looked for the disturbance, expecting to see a bobcat, an eagle, or maybe even a hawk or large owl, but they hid well if there were any. She decided to be more watchful in case it was an animal that would bother her.

As she drew further into the woods where the hot springs were, she felt a ripple of worry slither up her spine. The hair on the back of her neck stood up, and she tried to discount it, saying it was because she was going into the forested part of the ranch. She scoffed at her fears even as she listened for the cause of her discomfort.

As Kailani drew closer to the hot springs, she gave less attention to the thought that she was being watched and more to the natural wonder's inviting steam and warm water. If she and Seamus stayed together, really together, then she would not be sad to divide her time between South Dakota and the island of Hawaii. She loved Hawaii and would always call it home, but this was a beautiful second, if she were honest.

Kai swam and thought about her relationship with Seamus. He was more old-fashioned than she was used to and had definite ideas about how his life would go and, by extension, hers. His expectations for being a couple included him being in charge when there needed to be a specific leader. Kai wasn't used to that. Nor did she know how far that would go and how far she could allow it to go. Life was so complicated sometimes.

Her phone alarm went off, notifying her that the time for relaxing and pondering was over. Reluctantly, she lazed a little longer before the repeat of the missed notice drew her from the heated depths of the springs. The air around her was still warm enough to only bring a shiver due to a cool breeze rather than the steamy atmosphere around her.

Kai loved this hideaway but still needed something to do, so she planned her pathway to check the fence line. One of the guys mentioned that he wondered if there wasn't a break in the fencing because he'd had to get two cows from the back road this morning. Carter said the herd didn't often go in that corner of the pasture, so he thought they could last another day before going in search of the breach.

Kai decided to find the spot and then repair it. She'd feel like she was contributing, and that was something she needed. Seamus would be fine after the repair was done, a task her grandfather taught her long ago, but Seamus would not approve of it beforehand. That's why she didn't tell him, and her butt clenched at the thought of defying him. It was why she would only tell Carter after it was done.

Kai mounted Susie, who had enjoyed a lovely patch of grass and water in a small pond filled naturally by rain and mountain runoff. The water was crisp and clear. As they started further down the line to the area where the cows had gotten out, Kai had that eerie feeling that she was being watched again. She laughed it off and continued on. No one would be out in the middle of nowhere; that was where she was.

She slowly walked the fence line, singing to keep the worry from her mind until she found the break and pulled out her supplies to fix it. The herd became restless and jumpy enough to move in a huddled, skittish group. Kai had heard from the workers that there were bobcats, mountain lions, bears, moose, bighorn sheep, and more wandering around their barriers.

Kai was glad she'd gotten the mending supplies from a seasonal employee that didn't know she wasn't a ranch worker. He was new here, so seeing her everywhere reassured him that she was part of the ranch. He had no idea she wasn't supposed to do repairs. With the appropriate supplies and tools, she set to work repairing the broken wire, retightening it, and moving on.

And still, she felt the odd tingle up her back, making her neck hair stand on end, that alerted her to trouble. According to her family, no one had heard from Rufus in a week, which was something considering he had hounded them from the moment he discovered her missing until then. A week ago, he went radio silent, and damn if that didn't bother her more than knowing he was looking for her.

Kai wasn't one to borrow trouble, but she couldn't help but think her feeling of being watched was connected to his disappearance. Logically, none of that made sense, but in her fearful mind, it made loads of sense.

Unfortunately, she was unable to go the whole perimeter of the fence because it was getting cold, and darkness was coming. She gathered her gear and packed it, grabbed her empty bottle of water, and watched as the cattle in the far part of the pasture moved around restlessly.

With the darkness came the wildlife, so Kai returned to the saddle to head home. Susie fell into a brisk trot, but as the sun fell behind the trees, Kai worried that going faster was dangerous. She couldn't see the ground as well in the lessening light. She hadn't grown up here and didn't know where to go on instinct. However, Susie did, so Kai gave the horse her head and relaxed as they went straight home to the stable.

As she arrived, Renee said, "Wow, Seamus and Carter are really progressive. Fooled me."

Kai stopped and slid from the horse's back, pulling out the repair supplies in the saddle bag to be replaced. "What do you mean?"

"I mean that they allowed you to go out alone for the majority of the afternoon. That is something they have not allowed before. Not one of the Red Eagle men has allowed it. Ever. And were you fixing the fence? They never would have allowed that before you got here, citing the dangers of doing anything singularly. How did you get them to loosen the reins?"

"I didn't. I mean, it's always easier to ask forgiveness than permission, right?"

"So they don't know? If they find out, I bet you rethink your little mantra there."

"I'm not telling them."

"Good luck with that. Look, I would never tell, but," Renee shrugged, "just good luck."

"Wait, you have to finish that thought." Kai could feel her worry grow.

"All I meant was they have a way of finding out even if you don't tell them. It's the damnedest thing, but it doesn't look like any spies are around, so you may have gotten away with it. For now."

"Would you stop doing that."

"Sorry. You're right. Hey, gotta go. Dinner is in an hour. You might want to clean up and look like you were home all day, at any rate."

"Right."

In the shower, Kai remembered Seamus was very clear that when she left the safety of the lodge, house, or paddocks, she needed someone with her. She recalled his voice, clear as day.

"It's important to be as safe as possible. Accidents or animal attacks are more likely outside the daily living and working area. Also, there are spots of dead zones throughout the ranch. We've put up a booster tower at the back end of the acreage, but there are still some areas where you can't get reception."

She'd agreed to follow that rule but wanted to prove she could do it alone, just like other paniolos. Her traitorous conscience reminded her that even the cowboys and employees never went alone. Her feeling of doom was just as strong as the feeling that she was being followed and watched this afternoon. She'd keep that to herself, too.

Dinner was another lively session with the Red Eagles. Declan, as usual, allowed Teagan to talk up a storm, smiling at her antics, but he rarely entered a conversation for long. He was great at getting things going and then sitting back and listening to the banter. Kai imagined he got that from their father. Seamus' Até seemed to be a man of little words but enormous meaning, just like Declan. So when he was the one who asked her where she'd ridden, it surprised her.

"You look like a deer in headlights, Kailani." Seamus' use of her full name was not lost on her.

"Do I? Sorry, I was thinking about researching how to tell when a cow was ready to deliver."

No one said anything to that, and she didn't know if she was glad or concerned.

"Are you worried about the cows? Maybe the bison cows?"

Kai was honest when she said, "Maybe? At home, we just let them calve, but we don't have as big a spread or buffalo to deal with."

Stryker added, "I think we have something around here to help you figure that out. I'll sic Avery on it."

"Yes, he'll sic me on it because he doesn't know where anything is filed. Electronically or on paper," said his fiancée. Stryker leaned over and kissed her loudly. "Did you forget I'm your boss, baby? Be respectful."

"Of course, dear," said Avery with a complacent smile. "Whatever you say, dear."

"See what I put up with around here?" Stryker focused his statement on Kai.

"Yes," she commiserated, "I can see it is a hard life you lead."

Stryker moaned. "Corrupted already."

"I can spank her for you," offered Seamus with a laugh and a rubbing of her thigh.

"No," said Carter, "because if you spank one, you'll have to spank them all."

Declan sighed dramatically. "I've had a long day and don't have the energy for a discipline orgy tonight. Maybe another time."

"Good to know, Dec," said Teagan. "No sex tonight."

The room erupted into laughter, drawing back slaps from Callen and Stryker. Declan joined in the laughter. Carter shook his head.

"What did you ladies do today?" asked Callen.

"Read essays. I don't think I'll assign them anymore if I have to grade them. It's torture of the worst kind," complained Teagan.

"We were working on the upcoming events for the lodge," volunteered Avery, and she went on to discuss some of the community events planned for the winter. "Renee is great at just attending meetings and not volunteering for everything. Me? Not so much."

Kai needed the conversation to continue away from what she did today. "So, what do you do here during the winter? We get rain, but it must be incredible to see the snow. I hope I'll be here long enough to see it."

Silence again. Shoot. She took a bite and waited for someone to say something, anything. Seamus did. "You'll have plenty of opportunities to see the snow over this and future winters. I'm not letting go of you now that I've finally found you."

"I think I found you, big guy."

"Not sure either of you gets that prize exclusively," said Callen.

"Thought you were going on a date tonight," asked Seamus.

"I am. Dancing," answered Callen.

Renee laughed. "Too cheap to spring for dinner?"

"No, smartass, Bella doesn't get off work until six, and she wanted to go home first, so we'll go at eight."

Stryker stopped buttering his roll. "Bella Roundhouse?"

"Yes, and before you say it," Callen gave the room a hard stare, "she's changed."

Renee snorted.

"And that's enough out of you, young lady. Trust me to be smart enough not to get taken by a woman who was money hungry in high school."

"And after," murmured Avery.

"Avery, I'd have expected better from you." Callen was the fun-loving Red Eagle. He was rarely serious, but he was obviously serious about defending Bella.

Renee sighed and put a forkful of food in her mouth. Kai wondered if it was to keep from saying anything that would get Callen even more riled up.

"You're right. I'm sorry. If Bella has changed for the better, then I'm glad you're having fun with her." Avery's face turned red. "I mean not fun, fun." She turned even redder. "Never mind. I hope it's a great night... dancing."

Stryker chuckled as he pulled Avery over to hug her hard. "I think he gets it, baby."

Later, when the dishes were done, Callen left for his dancing date. The rest sat around in the family room and watched a movie. Afterward, they talked about Stryker's house that was in the planning and soon-to-be-built stage.

Declan nudged Teagan, who nodded. "Teague has an architect friend to finish the plans, so we thought we could set things up for our house in the spring. So it's done by the time Mam and Até are back. That way, the only thing we'd have to do is say the I Do's."

Teagan laughed and drew him down to her for a kiss. "You wish. The wedding is the hard part."

Stryker laughed. "So I'm told. Glad you're getting your house done early. That's two down, three to go. What about you, Shay?"

"Haven't thought too much about that yet. It's still early days for us." Seamus hugged Kailani. "When she says we're ready, then we'll be ready. Then I'll want the name of your friend, Teagan."

"Just have to ask."

Carter got up. "Well, I'll say my goodnights. It's been a long day, and I'd like to finish with a bang. I'll check on things as I go to the house. I'll see you all tomorrow. Oh, and Kai? If you're going out riding again tomorrow, can you exercise a few of the horses? We've got a couple that are getting used to the herd and they don't get as much exercise as the others."

"Um, sure."

"Appreciate it." With a long look at Renee, Carter grabbed his hat and headed out the door.

"You didn't mention you went riding today," Seamus said quietly.

"I wandered, is all. I'm bored with nothing to do, so exercising the horses fills my time."

"I know you're bothered by the downtime, baby, but that will change here soon."

"I know, it's just that I'm waiting on news from Nan and waiting on the season to change, waiting for more work. I seem to be waiting for everything."

"Hey," said Avery. "I want to go elderberry picking, and Stryker is in meetings all day. I'll set him up, and we can go late morning and have lunch on the mountain."

Stryker sat up. "You take your safety pack."

"What's that?" asked Kai.

Seamus answered. "It's a pack with emergency supplies and things you might need if you get caught in weather or surprise a predator or something."

"Oh, well, maybe I don't want to go with you, Avery. Besides, I don't have one of those packs.."

"You do want to go. Seamus can make you a pack. It's such a nice place to view the world from, and I've never seen anything up there except a few elk and deer," said Avery.

Teagan agreed. "Look, I'm a city girl for the most part, and I enjoy it. I'm just sorry I can't go too."

Renee frowned. "Bummer, I'm in some of Stryker's meetings, so I can't go either, but you'll have fun, and she's right. You need to see another aspect of the ranch and surrounding area."

"I'll make up your kit. I should have done it already, and you'll be ready to go." Seamus kissed Kai.

"Oka-a-y."

"We need to get to bed if we're going to get all this done tomorrow and get some exercising done with the horses." Seamus patted Kai's thigh indicating it was time to move.

Declan and Stryker both stood, reaching a hand down to their lady loves. "We need to head up, too," said Declan.

The women went upstairs to their rooms as the men walked around the house, closing things, shutting equipment down, and locking the doors for the night.

"Think I'll let Maverick out one last time before I turn on the alarm. You guys go ahead on up to bed. I'll finish this," said Stryker.

"Thanks," said Seamus as Stryker opened the door. Seamus took the stairs two at a time to catch up with Kai. Declan was just starting up the stairs when Seamus closed his door.

Maverick was out in the yard about a minute when he started barking his head off, waking up the entire ranch. Stryker grabbed his rifle, stepped onto the large country porch, and tried to locate the dog. When he did, it looked like Maverick had someone or something hemmed up in the corner of the shed next to the house. His mother's personal storage spot.

Declan, followed by Seamus and all the women, came down the stairs.

"What's going on?" asked Seamus as he accepted the shotgun Declan handed him.

Seamus walked to the door, and Declan followed. Seamus heard a shout from across the yard and knew it to be Carter.

The women followed the men as they walked out on the porch. Stryker looked over and said, "Girls get in the house."

"This isn't the wild west," complained Teagan.

"Besides, I'm as good a shot as you are," said Renee.

"That may be," said Stryker, "but if you all don't get your butts inside, I'll be spanking every one of you when we're done here. And you know I can do it."

Kai looked at Stryker's face and his arms. Yes, there was no doubt he could do it without any hardship. She backed into the house.

Declan spoke clearly, his deep voice resonating through his words. "And if you don't get back upstairs, I'll be the next one in line to take a crack at your back sides. Now move."

Both men never waited to see if the women listened. They expected them to do as they were told. Kai couldn't believe she was going back upstairs. No one would have been able to get this kind of compliance if she didn't want to give it. Living with Seamus on this ranch was changing her. She liked her man to take charge, but she wouldn't admit it. Kai knew she wasn't the only one, either. The women sat at the top of the stairs. But there were limits.

Maverick stopped barking. There was a gunshot. Seamus cussed, and the men talked, then nothing. The next thing Kai heard was the door open, and women scattered to the railings. The door closed, the alarm was set, and the gun cabinet was opened and closed. Then the men headed their way. Kai studied Seamus.

Stryker looked up and shook his head. "Get to bed, Avery Rose, and you too, Saoirse Renee."

"No," said Renee, "Not until you tell us what happened out there. Was there a bear or cougar?"

Stryker seemed frustrated. "Can't say what it was. I hope it was a four-legged creature, but honestly, I don't know."

Kailani asked. "Then what did you shoot at?"

"We didn't shoot," said Seamus as he pulled Kai into his arms, kissing the top of her head.

"It was Carter," said Declan. "He thought it was a cougar at first, but then, he wasn't sure. He shot over its head but then wondered if it wasn't a man crawling out from under the house. At any rate," continued Declan, "we can go to bed. Nothing to worry about. We turned on the gate security."

"Is Carter okay?" asked Renee.

Seamus answered her as he pulled Kai into his arms, heading toward their room. "Yep, fine. He's probably sleeping by now, which is where we all should be. Maverick's mad he didn't get to chase whatever or whoever it was."

Soon after climbing into bed, Seamus pulled Kai close and said, "You're not to do what you did today."

She snuggled in closer. "What do you mean?"

"I saw you ride off and stay gone too long. You didn't text anyone, and then you walked the fence for a while."

"What? How do you know?"

"Baby, this ranch is wired for sound. Nothing goes on here that you don't cross a camera or trip an alarm at some point. I have two screens for a reason. One to work on, one to show me all the camera feeds. Of which, in case you don't believe me, there are fifteen. They cover a pretty broad area. The fence is the main focus and the gates."

"Well, damn. I thought you said there are dead spots."

"Sure, but I have a cell tower to avoid that as much as possible, so the security can access data. And you're getting a spanking in the morning for it."

"Oh, no. I don't consent."

"Honestly, you have already given consent by previously engaging in the activity, but if you insist on withdrawing the consent, then I guess orgasms are out. You let me know if you change your mind in the morning."

Chapter Sixteen

Kailani

K Well damn. Kai was so horny she could scream. Seamus had edged her all night. He went at it hard at first, then he pulled her in tight and went to sleep. She was woken up twice more to his clever tongue and talented fingers working her up again, only to leave her hanging amid her need. She was exhausted but so sexually charged she slept restlessly.

The final straw was this morning when he said, "I'm sorry baby, that was mean of me. Let me make it better."

And then he proceeded to edge her again. His kisses were epic, and his caresses were carnal; he still didn't bring her off. It had to be cruel and unusual punishment. Then she ate breakfast with his roaming hand that was just under the radar. If he made one sudden move, it would be all over, and the room would know. He was a sadist.

"I'm going to exercise the horses," she said.

"I'll walk out with you."

She didn't want him to go with her. Spanking would be almost better than this. Almost. As she walked toward the stables, Seamus snagged her by the waist.

"Ready to get your spanking over and done with, or do you need more edging?"

"I don't want more edging, but I don't want a spanking. Edging is a horrible punishment by itself."

"Nope, edging is sexual excitement; not coming is punishment."

"You can't punish me twice for the same thing."

Seamus nodded. "True. So which is it? Edging or spanking?"

"Neither, thank you."

"Now that is a problem. You know daddy punishes for naughty and you have been very, very naughty.. Spanking is my preferred way to punish."

"I have not. Besides, you don't spank any other employees."

"True. Stryker and Declan spank the other female employees eligible for this perk. Renee has a deal." He led her into his office, closing and locking the door behind them.

"Okay, but if you don't spank your employees, then you can't spank me. That's discrimination." Her hands landed on her hips. "I could sue you."

"You're right. You're fired. Now bend over my desk."

"What?" Her hands dropped from her waist.

"You heard me. You are my primary concern, so if I spank for disobeying the rules and I can't spank employees, then you can't be my employee. So, you're fired."

"But you can't fire me because I won't let you spank me."

"Hmm. Okay, then, how about this. You're fired because we don't have anything for you to do for another couple of weeks, and we shouldn't pay for nothing."

"Damn it, you used my words against me."

His broad grin flashed and then was gone. "So, edging or spanking?"

"I want Renee's deal."

"Trust me, you don't. Besides, that isn't an option on the table. It's time to decide, Kailani."

"But edging is wrong if I'm your employee." Her hands landed on her hips again.

"Not if you're my baby girl and my employee. People do it all the time."

"Only around here."

"Then the precedent has been set."

"Besides, it's unethical."

"You're stalling, baby." Seamus took a deep breath and let it out slowly. "Kailani, I'm going to spank your ass because... You. Are. Mine. I want you to follow the safety rules. I have to trust you will do your best to stay out of harm's way. Otherwise, I'll have to wrap you in bubble wrap and put a minder with you. Your own bodyguard. If you want me to fire you first, so be it, but this punishment will happen."

She folded her arms across her chest. "Seamus."

He kissed her. "Bend over my desk, baby."

She stamped her foot.

"Cute, but don't do that again unless you want more."

He leaned in and unsnapped her jeans, slowly lowering the zipper. She didn't stop him. He considered that a good sign. Seamus slipped his hands inside both sides of the waistband and slid panties and pants down to her knees avoiding the strong impulse to stop and drop down to play between her creamy caramel thighs. He pulled her tight to him and rubbed her backside until it was warm.

Kai moaned. His baby loved ass play of any kind. She also loved spanking in ass play and sex in general, but she never wanted to admit it. He was okay with that if she allowed him full access. He swatted her butt while holding her close, his lips on hers. She whimpered. He slipped his finger into the wetness between her thighs, and she gyrated. His girl was drenched, and he had done that to her. All that edging had served a couple of purposes.

"Wet for me, lover?"

"No, but wet for an orgasm my mean man didn't give me? Yes."

Seamus chuckled. "I'll have to talk to him."

"Yes, you do. Tell him he's supposed to take care of me, not torture me."

"I'll need to figure out just what that means so I deliver the right message. Now was it the exciting you that was torture, or—"

"You are so sadistic, so horrible."

Seamus continued to lightly spank and massage her bottom cheeks to entice her. He put her over his desk. His finger returned to her wet core and then to her back entrance. She cried out when he introduced his digit without much fanfare. Her squeal was more in surprise and then desire than any tweak of pain. He played with her anus until she desperately needed to come.

"Tell me you know you were naughty to break the rules." She whined in her resistance. "Kai, does daddy have to get mean again?"

"No, I want to come." She wiggled her bottom.

"Spanking first. Here it comes."

Seamus slapped her backside fast and furiously. She whimpered, wiggled, and bounced but didn't fight him. Kai knew as well as he that she wouldn't last long after he heated up her backside, so he dropped his pants quickly and slammed into her hot core. After pounding in and out, he knew she was not quite letting go. He pulled out and pushed into her anus with firm slow insistence. If she had resisted, or hadn't been dripping and he hadn't had so much liquid excitement transfer, he would have needed lube, but there was plenty of natural lubricant. Most women needed clit action, and Kai would come with that, but today his girl needed ass action.

"Ahh, it hurts."

"It feels good." He slapped her ass. "Don't lie to daddy when he is trying to bring you off."

"So good, daddy, so good."

She arched and clamped down so hard on his penis that he wasn't sure the blood was flowing. The burning shot up from his balls into his shaft, and his whole lower half went into a frenzy of chasing that elusive orgasm. He pumped harder, faster, deeper. And then it hit. Like Kai had done, he froze for a moment, the sensations washing over him like an enormous tidal wave. He pumped until there was nothing left to release.

Seamus leaned over, kissed her damp neck, and touched her clit firmly. She shot like the proverbial cannon with a loud cry. There was nothing sedate about his lady. His shaft felt the squeezing a second time, but nothing could beat that first orgasmic clasping of his cock. He reached over and gave her some tissues.

"Let me take care of... shit."

"What?"

"No condom."

She froze a moment and then shrugged. "Well, you weren't inside for long, and you released, um, elsewhere. We can't change it now. I took my last pill yesterday, so hopefully, it will carry over today. Besides, if you were going to mess up, this was the right time of the month."

"Well, you're going to be naughty again, and I might lose myself in the sexiness of you being spanked, so you'd better go grab another month's worth. I'll bring a supply of condoms to my office."

"Or get a year's worth."

He watched her rub her backside and decided not to stop her. She had been punished enough, but a warning would be in order.

"Rubbing gets you more swats. Comfort at your own risk."

She pretended to ignore him and rubbed one more time to show her autonomy. "I have to go."

"Where are you going again?"

"Nowhere alone, so don't worry. I'm going to the horse barn, then the stables, to exercise a few horses before Avery comes out."

Seamus hesitated, then kissed her gently but with staying power. If he kissed this woman every time he thought of her, it wouldn't be enough.

"Wow," Kai said as he lifted his head, "That was nice. Who would have ever known that it was sexy to be gentle."

"Hey, I've been gentle before. Are you saying I wasn't sexy?"

She grinned, her eyes twinkling with merriment. "You are so confident in most areas of your life, but let me hint that you might have come up lacking at any time with me, and you're up in arms. Silly man, I love you no matter how you are."

Seamus stared at Kia hard. "I don't want to point out the obvious, but you just said you loved me."

"I did not; if I did, it was a slip."

Seamus smiled. "A Freudian slip, possibly, but you did say it, and I'm going to hold you to that."

"Don't put so much stock in words. It's actions that speak louder."

"I think your actions speak for themselves too."

Instead of replying to that statement specifically, she deviated. "Speaking of action, I have to go if I want to get anything done before Avery is ready to leave."

"Okay, I'll let you go for now. Your safety kit is on the front entry table in a green backpack. Don't forget it, or I won't be gentle when I address your disobedience."

"Only children disobey, Seamus, and you can't punish me for forgetfulness."

He laughed. "Don't count on it, woman."

"Seamus, I'll be fine.

"Kai, I'm serious here. We don't know where this Rufus Paolo is. I don't want to find out that he has discovered where you are before we can track him down. Any word about where he is?"

"Nan says no one has heard from him for a week, but he could be laying low. He'll never find me here."

"I should have tracked the asshole down. Waiting may have given Paolo the upper hand. I might need to go on a hunt. So be safe."

"I will. Promise. Have a good day."

She leaned in for her kiss but yelped at his slap on her thigh, followed by a quick peck.

"Mind me."

She opened her mouth to protest but decided against it. Her man was already standing, arms crossed, and his brow dipped low. Any challenge might end with her being banned from going. Better to leave things as they were than start a fight she knew she wouldn't win. Besides, wondering where Rufus had gone was at the forefront of her mind now.

After exercising two horses, Kai went inside, gathered the scrumptious, not-too-healthy lunch she and Avery had thrown together, grabbed water and her safety kit before meeting her friend at the four-wheeler. It was faster, and Kai had had her fill of riding for the morning. Her butt had felt every jolt in the horse's gait because of Seamus' protest of her choices this morning. She wanted to avoid that happening again. Avery pulled out a cushion from a storage bin in the four-wheeler and handed it over.

"I imagine you've had enough ass torture today between Seamus and the horses."

Kai sighed in relief. "How did you know?"

"I've been with Stryker for months, remember? And I grew up in this community. We all have heard rumors about the Red Eagle men. Renee showed me the cushion once when I needed it."

Kai shared a wry smile. "My sympathies."

"Thanks." The women laughed. "Now I'll drive because I know the best place for elderberries. Stryker showed me when we went for summer berries this year."

"Wow. Then let's go."

SEAMUS

Seamus decided to make a call for any updates from Kai's grandmother. He wanted to ask questions that Kai wouldn't like.

"Aloha, Aka Lodge."

"Mrs. Aka, this is Seamus Red Eagle. Kailani is fine."

"Thank you for leading with that. We are worried for her safety."

"Is there news?"

"News? Has Rufus shown up there?" His stomach dropped at the question. "Mrs. Aka, don't you know where Rufus is?"

"No, I told Kai that he has disappeared. We haven't heard from him or seen him in a week, maybe more. Didn't she tell you? Is he there?"

"No, he isn't here. Yes, Kai told me, but I thought I'd check again to see if anything had changed." He wanted to avoid causing the woman more concern, so he lied. His Kailani would love to capitalize on that bit of information except she hadn't told him and that was serious.

"Is my granddaughter there?" Mrs. Aka's concern was evident in her voice.

"No, ma'am, she isn't in the room, but she is on the ranch. She is out on a picnic with my sister-in-law."

Mrs. Aka sighed. "I know she missed not having a sister. Brothers are fine, but better with a sister."

"Yes, my sister is the only girl, and she would agree." He prodded her hoping to bring the elder back to sharing the update.

Mrs. Aka sounded distressed. "I heard just today that Rufus knows where Kai is. I don't know how, but Keith, our gardener, does work with Clifton Paolo on special occasions. Rufus' parents had a party for their anniversary last night. Anyway, Keith went to retrieve his vases and things this morning. He overheard Paolo talking to what sounded like his son on the phone."

Seamus' stomach cramped. "What did he say?"

"Something like 'Finally. If you know where the runaway bitch is, grab her and stop in Vegas. I don't care how guarded she is. And make sure she marries you before she gets back, or make it so she never comes back. But whatever you do, do it fast. People will notice you are gone if you stay away much longer.'"

Seamus was immediately alert and then asked suspiciously, "How did he remember so much?"

She sounded a little offended that Seamus asked but replied with her pride showing. "He carries a notepad so that he doesn't forget the tasks he has, or the instructions given. He just pulled it out fast and wrote it all down."

"Smart. Better keep that employee."

"He's been with us for more than 20 years."

Seamus nodded to the voice on the phone. He knew what good employees were worth. "I have to go now and round up Kai. When I find her, I'll have her call you. Thank you for talking to me."

"You take care of my granddaughter, young man."

"I will, Mrs. Aka. I promise."

Seamus got on his cell phone to Renee, who started to call his brothers and Carter. They met in the supply barn's office. As he gathered his gear, he waited for the others.

"I'll tell you what's going on, but you'll have to gather your hunting gear and survival packs as I talk. Make sure you're armed and ready for action."

When everyone arrived, they listened to what was happening, and Stryker ran down the list of gear needed for a check.

"Medical supplies."

Callen, who was good at medical things, called out, "Got it."

Seamus swore and began to walk out, but Declan stopped him. "Deep breath, man. You can't get out there and find you don't have what you need. I know this is hard, but there isn't any other way. We have to start slow to finish on top."

Seamus gritted his teeth. "Kai has no idea he's found her. They are in real danger, Dec."

"How the hell could he have found her?" asked Callen.

"That servicemember asshole, who I later learned was the cousin to Paolo, must have told him."

"No shit?" asked Declan. "Do I need to call Teagan's brother for more help? And what about Jacob? He's got skills and knows this land like the back of his hand."

"No time. If we can't find Kai and Avery quickly or things go south, then we'll call Wilder."

Stryker added. "Jacob is already planning on arriving today, so he'll be another Red Eagle to put into play if we need to."

"Good to have family here for added protection," said Callen.

Renee arrived fully loaded. "Let's go."

"I appreciate it, sis, but I can't risk you too." Seamus was adamant with his arms crossed in front of him. He was not going to argue.

"You aren't. You protested, I heard and disregarded. Now let's go."

Carter started toward Renee, and Stryker grabbed his shoulder to stop him.

"Renee," said Stryker, "I need you to fill Chaps and the rest in on what's going on and organize them. I also need someone to keep Teagan safe and watch the security feeds. No one else can do that except us, so you are the default."

Renee struggled with the shift in her duties but finally nodded. "Bring everyone home safe, Stryker."

"This fucker might know she's in our town and even on our ranch, but we know our land. We got this," said Seamus. His body was so tense he had to mentally talk himself down.

Carter maintained the all-terrain vehicles, so he assigned the use. He slapped Seamus on the back. "We'll find her. Seamus and Callen take the UTV because you might have to bring her home and need more space if she's hurt. The rest of us will jump on a few ATVs. Tell us where we're going, Seamus."

"I think they were going elderberry picking."

Stryker jumped on a vehicle. "I know where that is because I showed the best spot to Avery. And we all know where the best area for that is, so we head in that direction."

The men hustled. Guns, ammo, extra blankets in case someone got hurt, water, and some protein bars if they were out longer than anticipated. They all knew the drill. Their father and, later, the military had taught some of them the discipline to hold fire, but it was Até that insisted they all know how to handle a gun, shoot straight, and be responsible at a young age. Até had pounded into his boys, "Never take a human life unless necessary for your survival, but if deemed necessary, shoot to kill."

Richard Red Eagle made sure that his children, his cousin's boy Jacob and Stryker's best friend, Carter, knew the rules, and he had them practice ad nauseam, but it worked. Renee was just as good a sharpshooter as any of the boys, save Seamus. Both Renee and Stryker had taught Avery, so there was comfort in knowing that. Kailani had never held a gun that he could remember. Seamus had a natural eye, a steady hand, and concentration that could close out anything around him. His focus and patience came in handy when flying teams in and out of danger.

Seamus took the lead at first, but since they all knew where they were going, the men drove in like the cavalry. Time to take this fucker down, and Seamus prayed it wasn't too late for his girl. He loved her and couldn't imagine life without her. A hand hit his head.

"Watch ahead. Let the others on the ATVs go into the brush first. It'll help smooth the way for us," said Callen.

He wanted to go in first, not to lead the way, but to get to the girls just one millisecond faster, to know they were okay, just that much earlier. But Seamus nodded, knowing Stryker was just as anxious to get to them as he was. Hell, he had to keep his head in the game, or they wouldn't get in and out fast enough. He wasn't going to risk the girls' safety by being stupid.

Time to hyper-focus on the mission. Get in, get the girls, get out. Lock it down. Go on the hunt. Maybe they should call down to Wyoming and grab Teagan's brother. If things went too slow, he'd call in the sheriff. The more good men to eradicate this vermin, the better.

The others pulled ahead of him and cut into the trail. It was easy to see that this was the path Avery and Kai had driven because she was smart enough to bring an ATV rather than the horses. Quicker in and out if needed. Besides, his Kai's backside had to have been sore, and after exercising a few of the horses this morning, she'd likely been offered Renee's emergency cushion she thought no one knew about.

He smiled, and his heart nearly seized with the need to hold Kai and make sure she was unharmed. The forest was getting thicker here with more under-brush. They would do controlled burns for some years and take machetes to the old-grown. It must have been a few years because it was all high enough to smack him in the face if he didn't duck often.

They were getting close. A rifle fired, then Avery's return fire with her 257-bolt action rifle that she used for just about anything on the ranch. The scream arrived a few seconds delayed. The guys stiffened visibly in the machines ahead of him. Shit. Stryker was in the lead and executed a few hand signals while the others branched off the trail in two directions. Stryker stayed on the pathway. Seamus stayed behind him. He knew Stryker thought that the fastest way was through the middle, and that's where he was going. Seamus agreed.

Another shot and another return from Avery. Then silence. They were so close Seamus wanted to jump off his vehicle and run. No, the others were coming in from different angles hoping they could flush the asshole out.

The trees cleared to a small meadow. Avery was near the ATV, tied up, and Kai was... lying on top of someone with Maverick in the mix, legs everywhere.

Chapter Seventeen

Kailani

"Get down!" yelled Avery.

Searing heat made a line across her upper arm. "I think I'm shot. I mean, it's hot and hurts like hell." Warm blood seeped through her sleeve, and she could feel it roll down her arm. "I'm bleeding."

"Shit! Okay, roll under the UTV. The shot came from up in those higher elevations, so they won't likely see you from above the vehicle. I wish Stryker was here."

As she rolled underneath, Kai whimpered. "Me too, and Seamus. It hurts. There's blood everywhere. What are we going to do?"

"We're out of cell range here. We're going to have to send up a flare."

"Seamus said they have a tower that extends cell service across the ranch."

"This is still a dead spot. We're in the ridges between mountains. A flare is our best bet."

"But what if they don't see it."

"Then we send up another one."

Kai hissed when she moved again. Another shot, and Avery returned fire. Now what?

Kai reached into her pack to see what was in there to help with the bleeding, and she pulled out a phone. "Avery, I have a phone in my pack."

"What? Seamus must have put in his satellite phone. Call the ranch."

Kai found the number programmed in. Kai called the ranch and heard from Renee that help was coming but would it be too late?

Kai had never been more scared in her life. The sound of motorized vehicles could be faintly heard. They were still at a distance but were coming in their direction. This would soon be over. The relief was short-lived as another bullet pinged off their ATV. Kai was thankful they had stopped on the edge of the forest, close to a small amount of undergrowth. That tuft of vegetation kept them hidden from the sight of Rufus. They just had to hold on a few more minutes.

Rufus must have had the same idea, for he grabbed his gun and shot again. Avery didn't fire back. She didn't want to risk hitting Maverick, who had bounded through the woods and stopped just short of the clearing. Kai couldn't swear to it, but Seamus' dog gave every appearance of assessing the situation and working on a solution. He kept just out of sight of Rufus.

"Kai, can you hear the guys coming?"

"Yes. They aren't far."

"Good," said Avery. "The gunfire has dulled my hearing. It will come back when this is over."

In that moment, Kai grew to love Avery. She was scared, that was obvious, but she had skills and wasn't going to allow Rufus to kill them if she could help it. Kai had never shot a gun in her life. She had no need to, so when Avery had pulled out a shotgun from beside her in the SUV,, Kai was shocked. And thankful.

Things were unnervingly quiet. Kai trembled with the unknown of the situation. She knew where Rufus was and what he was doing when shooting or shuffling about, but he'd stopped both. Maverick was still focused in the same general area Kai knew Rufus was in, so she trusted he was still far enough away to not grab them.

"Avery," Kai whispered.

"What?"

"Maverick is poising to jump. We have to be ready to grab his gun or run when he does. Which is it?"

"I think we grab his weapon so he can't shoot at us any longer and then run."

Kai's arm still hurt, but she blocked out the pain and burning. It wouldn't be the only thing in pain if Rufus got her, so it was time to take control. If they could.

"Right. I'll go for the gun if you keep him covered."

"You sure?"

"No, but does it matter?"

"No."

Kai carefully rolled out from under the ATV but didn't stand up. She contemplated her movements when Maverick attacked. The dog had an uncanny ability to wait for the perfect time. Suddenly, the time had come, and the shepherd leaped on Rufus, his body in a tightly bunched killer mode. She'd never seen this side of Maverick before, but this was killer controlled chaos.

Rufus yelled and screamed as Mav bit and fought him.

Kai flew across the ground with Avery beside her. Rufus shot, and time stood still for a millisecond as they waited to see if the bullet hit its target, but it didn't. Time was set back in motion. Maverick continued to tear at Rufus, and Kai grabbed the gun, dragging it away from him.

Avery swung the butt of her gun and nailed Rufus in the head. Somehow, Kai didn't think that was the best idea. Couldn't the gun have gone off? But it didn't, so she didn't have time to contemplate the safety of that act. Rufus stumbled to the ground. Kai gave the gun to Maverick, who had backed up when Avery clobbered Rufus. The dog started to drag the long weapon backward, out of the way.

In two seconds, Rufus must have realized his gun was being dragged off by the dog and made a dive for it, landing on it. Kai tried to overcome him enough to allow Maverick to continue to take the gun, but once the loyal dog saw Rufus was on her, he stopped grappling for the rifle and headed to protect her.

Arms, legs, and dog were in a chaotic tumble. Rufus allowed the dog to separate him from Kailani, changing his focus for the rifle. He rolled and grabbed the gun this time. He turned it toward Kai. Where Avery was, Kai didn't know for sure. Her focus was on saving Maverick and not dying. Hopefully, Avery was under protective cover. Rufus turned his weapon toward Maverick, and Kai did the only thing she knew would send the dog in the opposite direction.

"Get Seamus. Mav, go get Seamus."

Kai dove at Rufus who hadn't stepped far enough away to be unreachable and in that distraction, the dog shot off like a light in the direction he had first come. At least he wouldn't die today. Rufus shifted his gun to Kailani. As she lay on the ground, she wished she could have the same assurances. Kai saw some movement in the edge of her peripheral vision, and she was glad that men had less developed sight than women.

"Time to quit fucking around, Kailani Aka. If you don't come with me, you won't go with anyone. Am I clear?" He looked at Avery. "Toss the gun. You're pretty. Too bad I won't have time to have some fun before I leave you."

"Why won't you leave me alone?"

"Matter of principle now. I not only want the ranch, but I want you to suffer. You led me on what my mother called a 'merry chase.' It was fun at first, but I grew tired of your games. Time to hand over the spoils. Now, tie her up."

Rufus shook a length of rope in Avery's direction, then held it out to Kai.

The ATVs must have passed them because there was no more engine sound. Their chance for rescue was gone. She was going to be brave and do the best she could to save Avery. If tying her up was what had to happen to ensure that happened, then that's what she would do. Kai decided to try another angle. Anything to gain some control. Kai didn't look in Avery's directions because if the woman was frightened it wouldn't help Kai's bravado stay in place.

"There are cameras."

"I got in, didn't I?" he laughed cruelly.

"Pure luck, but I guarantee, someone is watching the cameras now. Unless you walk the exact same path, and your luck holds, you won't leave unnoticed. And now that Maverick is looking for his master, the whole state will be looking for you. And me. Better you just head out now."

"I can't leave without you, and she knows what I look like."

"Don't be ridiculous. Everyone knows what you look like. The whole ranch has your face in their mind. The sheriff and his office all know what you look like. Hell, even the people in Cattleman's know your face."

Rufus looked a little wild as the realization settled into his gut.

"Look, if you leave her alone," Kai indicated Avery with the toss of her head, "I'll go with you. I can pave the way by telling them I chose to go with you."

The sound that came from Rufus could only be described as maniacal. Had he lost his mind, or was he this evil? "I don't want you, you stupid bitch. I want what your grandparents have. The ranch. My father wants it, and what he wants, he gets. But not this time; I'm taking what I want. I did all the work, so if my father wants it, he'll pay handsomely for it. Now tie her up, or I shoot you both right here. It would save me from dragging around extra baggage. And with you gone," he stared at Kai, "I only have to prey on their devastation, and they will sell."

"They won't sell to you."

"Well, that would be unfortunate because I'll just have to help them meet with some unfortunate life events, won't I? The last man standing will sell. I guarantee it."

Avery said, "My fiancé and his brothers will be here soon, and when they do, your safety won't be in the bag anymore."

"Tie her up, or I'll just shoot her now. Your choice, Miss Aka. We need to leave."

"Why take me? I'll only be trouble."

"Because I need you to marry me before I kill you. That is the whole reason for all of this; to put me in the line of succession. I know the will you have, the kind you all have. A spouse must either personally work the land or purchase their share. I'll purchase it, but I need that marriage certificate before you die to put things in place."

Avery cut her eyes to the pack that held their safety kits. Kai gave a very slight nod. The kind she'd seen the guys give each other. Avery's stare was full of meaning. She walked over to the woman.

"Kick that gun out of her reach," said Rufus. "Hurry, I have a schedule, and you are slowing me down." Why hadn't Avery used it when she had the chance? Too frightened probably.

"Kai," Avery whispered when the women were close. "I put a pocketknife in the front inside pocket of my vest. You can make out like you are tying me up but slice the rope where it won't all fall off."

She nodded and did as Avery instructed. These women were resourceful. She sliced through the rope when he wasn't looking, too busy ranting. This thing was sharp!

She was careful not to push the gun too far away from Avery in case she needed to use it again and turned back to her captor, knife in her back pocket now. Her arm still hurt but forcing that to the back of her mind wasn't as hard as she'd thought it would be. Guess the mind prioritizes when you're in danger.

There was shuffling in the brush beyond, and Kai hoped that Maverick wasn't back. She prayed it was the guys. Kai knew she couldn't go with Rufus, and Avery needed a distraction, so she moved to a place that encouraged Rufus to change his focus from Avery's direction to the trail. Mav came out of nowhere and attacked Rufus again, who was no more prepared for this action than the first.

"Ah! Get off me!" he said. Maverick was focused on the arm holding the gun. It soon slipped from his hand to the ground.

Rolling to his knees, her stalker lunged for Kai, who had turned to check on Avery.

"Kai!" Avery yelled.

Kai grabbed her knife and was relieved it flipped open like a switchblade. She screamed and instinctively plunged her weapon into his body. The sickening feeling of the blade sliding into flesh, going to the hilt, was horrific. She didn't let go of the steel defender, drawing it back out of his body.

Massive bodies stampeded out of the woods, swarming the little picnic area. Stryker had Avery in his arms. Kai was safe in the arms of Seamus, which was all she would ever need. But more than Red Eagles were here.

"Where did all these people come from?"

Seamus, who wouldn't let go of Kai, said, "Meet the Sheriff Cantrell. Looks like he brought the whole office to this party. Appreciate it, Sheriff."

Sheriff Cantrell walked over to the Red Eagles, all standing close together. "Should have known you could handle it but, the law being what it is, figured I'd better take a look to make sure you boys were fighting fair. Howdy ma'am. I figure you must be what all the fuss was about. Fritz Cantrell, at your service." The sheriff reached out his hand and there was a rumble in Seamus' chest.

"Nice to meet you and thank you for coming. My name is Kailani Aka but I'm sure you know that." She smiled and the sheriff's face lit up. Seamus pulled her closer.

"I'm going to need to ask you and Ms. Avery questions about what happened here." Fritz looked at the Red Eagle men, and cleared his throat. "But I can do that when you have relaxed a little and are in more comfortable surroundings. Would tomorrow morning be okay? I'll come to you."

"Kai sighed in relief. "That would be so appreciated. Thank you for being so accommodating."

Fritz looked at the men. "And all of you better be in attendance with the ladies. I need to hear your side of this story."

Stryker was the first to reach out his hand. "Thanks, Fritz. I know you're busy." The rest of the men followed suit. Seamus ended the round of handshakes with a heartfelt thanks.

"I know we don't call you often and we do like to handle things on our own, but we know, without a doubt, that if we need you, you will be here. Thank you."

The man turned a little pink and no one told him. It was enough to know he heard Shay's words. In a matter of minutes, once they were released to go home, the men started to gather the women's gear.

"Sorry, you can't touch that. We'll return it when we get it cataloged and pictures are taken," said the deputy. "I'm going to have to keep the shotgun."

Avery looked at Stryker and he nodded his consent.

"And the knife."

"I'm not sure where it is. I must have dropped it. I was standing in front of him the last time I had it." Kai shrugged. "Maybe you could check the ground."

"We are but I'm going to have to," he cleared his throat, "Um, pat you down to make sure you don't have it."

"The hell you will. I'll check."

"I'm sorry, Mr. Red Eagle, but you can't. I, um, will be careful."

Kai's hand touched Shay's forearm. "Shay, let the man do it and we will go home."

Carter cleared his throat with a hard grunt. "We'll meet you at the ATVs." The rest began to walk to where they left the machines and whistled for Maverick.

"Now, I'll be careful, Miss Aka."

The deputy reached forward to begin at her blue jeans pocket when another deputy yelled out, "Found the knife."

Seamus whipped Kai out of the deputy's reach so fast, the man was left for a second still reaching for the pockets.

"Thanks for the help. You'll let us know when we can retrieve our gear and the vehicle, yeah?"

"Oh, right. As soon as we can, sir. Have a better night."

Kai couldn't stop thinking about how this family had all put themselves on the line for her and her family. If she had any doubt about the love the Red Eagles had for others, she just had to remember how they saved Avery and took down Kai's stalker-turned-kidnapper before he could actually do more than scare them, before he killed her.

Seamus gathered her in his arms and held her tightly under the comforter. "Sleep, baby girl. Daddy has you. I will always have you. I love you."

"I love you so much."

"I know, baby, now sleep."

THE NEXT MORNING, WHEN the women got to the part where Maverick was attacking and Kai was trying to get the gun from Rufus, Kai asked Avery.

"Avery, why didn't you shoot the gun after we had gotten his gun? I mean you hit him on the head with the butt of the gun instead."

"You what?" Stryker sounded horrified.

Avery shrugged. "There were only two shots in the gun. I want a handgun from now on. It has more bullets."

They all laughed, and Kai suspected it was to relieve the tension. She needed to call Nan.

"Well, thanks everyone. Looks like this is cut and dried. We'll release your possessions in another few days or so. The knife, however, I'm going to have to keep. Sorry."

"I don't want it back anyway. I know I didn't kill him because I know enough anatomy to know there were no major organs and you arrived moments after it happened. So how is Rufus?"

"Well, it seems he's fine. And you're right, no major damage and he was released to us this morning with little to do but wait for him to heal. His family got him a good lawyer, but the man isn't firing on all cylinders, so there will be that to contend with. Anyway, thanks again. We'll call you back if or when we need anything else."

Epilogue

Seamus still had occasional nightmares or flashes of the fear he experienced when his last military mission went fubar. Still, his remembrances of Avery and his Kai, held at gunpoint by that madman, would haunt him forever. His imagination filled in all the blanks. South Dakota wouldn't only be Kai's new home. It looked like Rufus Paolo would be a guest of the state for a long time.

They all gathered in the office and called Até and Mam after the deputies left. It took some fancy talking to get Até to stay in Ireland and not come home.

"This is too much. I never should have agreed to spend a year away from the ranch and you all."

"Até, we're more than grown; honestly, we've handled it already, so what would you be returning to? Winter in South Dakota. So stay there with Mam, enjoy, and relax. Everything is calm now. But at least you can meet your future daughter-in-law," said Seamus.

"Another one?" asked Mam. "Put her on; we need to talk."

The next ten minutes were spent answering questions until Até said enough was enough. Jacob grabbed the phone.

"Até?" asked Jacob. "How are you?"

"Jacob! How are you? I'm so glad to see you at the ranch. I've always wanted it for you, and Stryker said you'd agreed to help with things."

"For now. I needed the break and to come home, so thank you for suggesting it."

"It was Stryker. I often suggest, but he only takes the good advice." Até laughed. Soon they ended the call, but the feeling of contentment swept across the room.

"Were you going to ask me or just assume it was true, Seamus Red Eagle? A girl likes—"

"A girl likes to be asked. I know and I'm sorry. The last twenty-four hours made me feel a little desperate."

Seamus reached into his pocket, and in the middle of his siblings and their fiancées, Carter and Shay's cousin Jacob, Seamus reached for Kailani's hand and dropped to one knee.

Looking deeply into her eyes, he said, "Kailani Aka, you are the most beautiful woman, inside and out, that I have ever known. You're the first person I think of every morning and the last thought I have before sleeping. Yesterday, when I knew you were in real danger, I almost lost my mind in worry and recrimination for not keeping you safe. I won't ever be happy without you, and if you agree to be mine forever, I promise to move heaven and earth to make you glad you did."

Grabbing the ring and opening up the box as though seeing the ring would help her decide, he asked, "Kailani, will you marry me?"

The tears were racing down Seamus' face as fast as they ran down hers. She reached her palm out to cup his cheek. He was almost the same height on his knees as she was standing, but that didn't matter. He was her everything.

"I will agree on one condition."

"Name it."

"You let me be a paniolo."

"Done."

"Really?"

"Yep. Just say yes."

"Yes."

The whoop that went up wasn't from Seamus because his lips and mouth were occupied with Kai's.

SEAMUS HAD BECOME QUITE open about his thoughts now that she had accepted his proposal. Kai was a paniolo, but not like she thought. She could have complained that Seamus had created a specific definition for paniolo. It involved the things Kai loved and none of the tough stuff. She was okay with that.

Her family lawyer was able to get an injunction against the Paolo family and a permanent order to keep them from the property and any member of their family. Now that the paperwork was all legal, Shay and Kai were preparing to take a trip to Hawaii to visit and pack her things.

Something was up with Seamus' cousin, Jacob. Renee said it was woman problems. Who knew? Hopefully, he could make things work for him because, in Kai's opinion, everyone should have someone.

She tried to be the good girl Seamus always admonished her to be. No more secrets and no more going behind his back... well, except when she went out with the ladies. That was an entirely different story.

"Time to go home, ladies," said Declan. He started gathering their coats and moving glasses from in front of them.

"Just a little longer, Dec. I'm not through with my drink."

Seamus sauntered over from the table the guys were at, nursing their beer and letting the women enjoy the night.

"Let's go, girls. We have church in the morning, and I don't need the minister eyeing us like the cats dragged us in. Mam would have a fit."

"But she won't know," said Kai.

"She has spies everywhere, baby."

As the women grumbled on their way out of Cattleman's, there were three distinct swats to swaying backsides and three grins on Red Eagle faces. Carter and Renee were at it again, arguing over something, and Jacob and Callen took up the rear, seemingly oblivious to the action preceding them.

Kai leaned into Seamus, and they exited the building. "I love you, Seamus Red Eagle."

"And I'm so in love with you, it scares me. I'm the luckiest man in the world."

Kai grinned. "You are."

Another swat landed on her backside. "I really am."

THE CAFÉ WAS FULL WHEN Renee joined Janna at the corner table.

"Wow, who left the flood gates open?" Renee asked.

"No clue, but it has something to do with the Rodeo heading to town in a few weeks."

"Is it that time already?" asked Renee as she reached for the menu.

"It is, but there must be more to it this year. I think they are bringing a bonus western show as an evening event. Brings in more people and more money." Tansy said. "My brother is excited to help organize it here on the ground."

"Well, we have something to organize ourselves," said Renee.

"What's that?"

"Callen is the last man standing."

"He is! I have to say, I thought your idea was crazy but when I watched each of the guys fall, even Seamus," Janna said with a pout, "I had to hand it to you. You have done a great job."

"Well, I honestly haven't done much but liked their choices and make the ladies feel comfortable. Now, with all of them engaged, it's time for Callen."

"He said he likes to hook up and then go home," Janna reminded Renee.

"So he might be a little harder, but he did mention a girl he went on a date with a month or so back. I don't really know her, but by reputation, which isn't good. Maybe I'll see how the temperature is in that direction."

"Good luck. I'm thinking he is going to go down a lot harder than the others."

"Maybe. And now that Jacob is here, we might need to work on him. Not sure, so I'll just keep an eye out. If he doesn't bug me, then no problem. He can remain single."

"Good luck. Now let's order. I'm starving."

The End

About the Author

Alyssa Bailey

USA Today and #1 Bestselling Author of Diverse Romance that is realistic and sensual with a touch of suspense. A dyed in the wool Texan living in Alaska for half her life, Alyssa now divides her time between the beauty of Southeast Alaska and the piney woods of East Texas. She enjoys taking from her own experiences to create series in fictitious worlds to tease the reader's palate and invite them to sink into exciting adventures.

Alyssa enjoys writing consensual power exchanges between intelligent, sassy women who are not afraid to make a stand and loving men confident enough to give his woman space but masterful enough to keep her safe despite her choices. There is *always* a happily ever after.

Follow me on Goodreads:
https://www.goodreads.com/author/show/14149220.Alyssa_Bailey
Visit me online and sign up for my Newsletter:
http://alyssabailey.com[1]
Join my Facebook Group for fun and prizes:
https://www.facebook.com/alyssabailey.romance
Find me on Social Media:
https://linktr.ee/alyssabailey

---

1. http://alyssabailey.com/

More Alyssa Bailey Romances

LORDS AND LITTLE LADIES: Regency Historical, Spicy
  Lord Thayer's Choice
  Lord Ashton's Decision
  The Black Laird Requires
  Lord Kendrick's Obligation

DARLING DUCHESSES: Regency, Daddy Dom, Spicy
  The Devil Duke's Little Distraction

CHASE ABBEY SERIES: Regency, Spicy, Suspense
  Lord Barrington's Minx
  Becoming Lady Barrington
  Lady Caroline's Defiance
  His Improper Lady

SAFE AND SECURE SERIES: Contemporary, Suspense, Spicy
  Saving Sharlee
  Saving Jessie
  Saving Ivy
  Securing Mallory
  Securing Callie
  Securing Becky (2023)
  Securing Finley (2023)

THE O'CONNOR SERIES: Contemporary, Rancher, DD, Spicy
  Liam & Jocelyn's Story

Her Sweet Complication
Liam's Lessons
Loving Liam

CIARÁN AND KATHERINE'S Story

His Gentle Persuasion
Rancher's Creed
Katie Consents

QUINLAN AND CHEYENNE'S Story

Quinlan's Quest
Accepting His Way
Her Balancing Act

KELLI AND PARKER'S Story

Meeting Her Needs
Kissing Kelli
Keeping Kelli

CIÁN AND MOLLY'S STORY

In Pursuit of Molly
Freeing Molly
Forever Molly

LONE WIND SERIES: Contemporary, Spicy, Native American

Reclaiming Clover

CLEARWATER RANCH TRILOGY -Contemporary, Spicy, Alpha
Piper's Plan
Camille's Second Chance
Josie's Refuge

TAMING TEXANNA-American Historical, Native American, Spicy
Cowboy Welcome- Contemporary, Spicy
In the Spirit of Christmas -Contemporary, Sweet

RED EAGLE RANCH- Contemporary, Rancher, Spicy, Multi-Cultural
Stryker's Girl (Book 1)
Declan's Girl (Book 2)
Seamus' Girl (Book 3)
Jacob's Girl (Book 4) (2023)
Callen's Girl (Book 5) (2023)
Renee's Reward (Book 6) (2023)

GUARDIANS OF REFUGE- Contemporary, Military, Spicy
SEAL of Refuge (Book 1)
The Strategy of Love (Book 2)
The Tactics of Love (Book 3)
The Mandate of Love (Book 4)

SAGE COUNTY
Deep Waters (Book 1)
Still Waters (Book 2)

ANTHOLOGIES (HEAT VARIES)

Sweet Town Love

Historical Heroes

Love, Christmas 2 Movies You Love

Love, Christmas 2 Recipes

FREE Book Bites 11

Irresistible Heroes

Tempting Protectors

Sexy and Seductive

Sweet and Sassy Summertime Vol. 2

Dear Santa: A Christmas Wish

Sweet and Sassy New Beginnings

MULTI-AUTHOR BOX SETS (Heat Level Various)

Love, Christmas 2 Recipes

FREE Book Bites 11

FREE Book Bites 13

Irresistible Heroes

Tempting Protectors

Sweet and Sassy Summertime Vol. 2

Dear Santa: A Christmas Wish

Sweet and Sassy New Beginnings (July 20, 2021)

Stateside Doms- Her Wyoming Dream Daddy

Don't miss out!

Visit the website below and you can sign up to receive emails whenever Alyssa Bailey publishes a new book. There's no charge and no obligation.

https://books2read.com/r/B-A-MXIL-NUFDC

BOOKS 2 READ

Connecting independent readers to independent writers.

Did you love *Seamus' Girl*? Then you should read *Stryker's Girl*[2] by Alyssa Bailey!

"You'll like your brothers again once they each find their true love. Their women will tame them for you."

Young adult, steady job, parents in Ireland for a year, sounds like heaven, right? Not to Saoirse Renee, who is bound by a promise to live at home with her four nosy, intrusive brothers. Their need to run her life with hot Irish tempers and immovable Nakota rules, has gotten completely *out of control.*

Renee, the youngest of five children born to an Irish-emigrant mother and a Nakota Sioux father, often finds reconciling her parents' worlds with her own challenging. The cultural diversity is, at times, explosive. Richard Red Eagle expected his sons to watch over their little sister, while his wife, Kayleigh, does damage control with their daughter.

2. https://books2read.com/u/38QyVL

3. https://books2read.com/u/38QyVL

With a little help from providence and some strategic orchestrating, Renee intends to help each of her brothers find their true love. She can smell sweet victory and see her freedom just around the corner. Time to get to work.

First victim on the list? The eldest: **Stryker.**

Read more at alyssabailey.com.

Also by Alyssa Bailey

Red Eagle Ranch
Seamus' Girl

Watch for more at alyssabailey.com.

www.ingramcontent.com/pod-product-compliance
Lightning Source LLC
Chambersburg PA
CBHW060228180626
46813CB00007B/3002